The Beautiful Dead Saga

Book 5

by

Daryl Banner

Join Daryl's Mailing List!

Be the first to hear about his latest releases
and get an exclusive sneak peek behind the scenes
of being an author!

www.darylbanner.com/subscribe.html

Are you a member of Daryl's Doorway on Facebook?

It's a place to have fun, chat about everything
Daryl Banner, and hear the latest book-world news!
It's totally top secret, but here's the way in:

www.facebook.com/groups/darylsdoorway

The Beautiful Dead Saga

Book 1
The Beautiful Dead

Book 2
Dead Of Winter

Book 3
Almost Alive

Book 4
The Whispers

Book 5
Winter's Doom

Book 6
Deathless

List Of Chapters

Prologue

1

Chapter One

Home

6

Chapter Two

A Grim Welcoming

21

Chapter Three

The Trial

39

Chapter Four

Death After Life

60

Chapter Five

An Ocean Of Faces

77

Chapter Six

Necrocite

97

Chapter Seven

So Much Dead

132

Chapter Eight

The Delivery

157

Chapter Nine

The Living World

186

Chapter Ten

Closing The Yellow Eye

212

Epilogue

235

Prologue

Anima.

I know the word. My sister knows the word. The Dead hiss and whisper and grunt upon the uttering of that vile, strange, beautiful word.

Yet here I sit, a glowing green stone in my palm, full of the theoretical stuff of Undeath, and I don't know how to use it.

Do I speak to it?

"Awaken," I growl, but my word is lost to the dead trees, the mist over my head, and the dark.

"Come to life," I command it, but the proud, green thing only stares back at me.

"Anima!" I demand tiredly.

Nothing and nothing.

When my sister comes through the trees to find me— her feet snapping the lifeless twigs, tiny bones, and dead things beneath them with every footfall—I always tuck my pretty treasure away at once. I don't know why, but I feel a great and terrible possessiveness over it, like I can't stand for the stone to be in anyone else's hands. I must protect it with my life.

Well, with my Unlife.

My Undeath.

My *whatever-one-might-call-it*.

Every time my sister comes by, she looks upon me with her one eye and her one empty eye socket, and she asks the same question: "Any sign of Winter?"

Winter.

My sister hasn't used her own name in a century, yet she remembers at once the name of the woman with the winter white hair.

Despite her name being *Jennifer*, my sister insists on the name *Winter* for the Living girl who came and left.

And when I give my inevitable grunt of *no*, my sister makes the same scowl, then murders her way through the deathly woods, muttering and grunting to herself as she picks irritably at the one or two hairs left on her otherwise bald head, disappearing.

And I'm left alone again with the green stone.

And my thoughts of *her*.

Winter. Jennifer. Whoever she is.

I close my eyes and hold the stone to my chest. I find myself wondering what my sister knew of that woman.

Winter's Doom

I've done this many times since Jennifer left this land on that giant metal bird in the sky, that creation of the Living, that thing that makes loud noises and cuts across the sky. Countless times I've held this stone, struggling to remember a thing I never knew.

Behind my eyelids, I see something for the first time—a camp.

My eyes flash open.

The dark woods surround me again.

What was that vision? What was that place?

I grip the stone tighter and clench shut my eyes once more, desperate to return there. And at once, the camp bursts to life before my closed eyes. I feel young, small, youthful. Am I a child? Did I die as a child?

I feel my sister's grip on my hand, tight and strict and protective—as protective as my own hold on this green stone right now—as we stroll together through the camp.

Where is this place? What is it?

The memory tries to fade, but I hold on with every ounce of me, desperate to see it to the end.

And at once, my real feet pick me up off the ground and I'm running through the dark woods with my eyes still closed, chasing the dream as if it was real, as if I was running toward the very camp itself. The brush is all unfamiliar—dead trees and crunchy grass and gritty air—yet the scent is eerily the same.

It's a deadly scent.

A nothing scent—all that the Dead can smell with their lack of the sense of smell.

At once, I feel the trees open around me. I'm in a clearing, yet my eyes remain closed. I inhale deeply, desperate to smell something, as if the memory itself gives off a scent I might track.

I see an army of Dead storming that camp. I hear the shrieks and cries of Living men, women, and children. A woman hides. A man hurls himself into a tent. Two children run into the woods, screaming.

One of the men stands against the Dead with a giant hammer in his hand.

John? Is that John, the man who came with Jennifer to this place?

Before I can have any opinion of it, my sister—my Living, two-eyed, full-haired sister—turns to me and cries out, "Run!"

I'm a slave to the memory, running the way my child self did, tearing into the woods with abandon. It isn't long before I realize my sister is no longer running with me, having fallen behind to protect the camp. I'm alone.

I call out my sister's name. No one calls back.

Then the child that is me looks up into the sky, terror in his heart—in *my* heart.

And with my Living eyes, I see the sun.

Winter's Doom

I've almost forgotten what it looks like. It isn't the eternal grey swirl of nothingness that us Dead see. No, with Living eyes, I see a beaming blue sky broken only by the reaching web of branches overhead, and a bright yellow circle of sunlight pouring over me.

Then the jaws of a Dead person whose name I'll never know find my face before I can even scream.

I jerk away from the memory, the green stone falling to the stony ground at my feet. I shake with terror as I back against a nearby tree, paralyzed with fear.

It was like a second Waking Dream, remembering at once what took me from that world to this one.

I peer up into the sky. It is only grey again.

Grey and dead as I am.

Was it due to the green stone that my memory of that day became so vivid? Was that stone responsible?

I snatch it right up from the forest floor, then stare into its depths once more.

And it's while peering into those depths, dark curiosity burning in my unbeating heart, that I see it for the first time, something new, something strange.

A face.

And in that green, glowing Anima, that face stares curiously right back at me.

Chapter One

Home

I stare into the dark, dull rock like a mirror.

I see nothing, of course, but it sure sometimes feels like something within it is staring back at me.

What is it with this dull, useless thing that has me feeling so … uneasy?

"What are you looking at, Jen?" asks John from the other side of the train car, his voice deep and suspicious.

I pocket the dark, ugly item at once. "Nothing."

"Was that the rock we took from the gardens?" There is little that ever escapes John's attention. "Why do you still hold on to it? I thought we were putting all of that Undead crap behind us."

"We are."

"So why—?"

The intercom on the train cuts him off. "Arriving soon. Prepare for departure."

His half-asked question is left unanswered as I rise from my seat to gather the few belongings I brought.

Winter's Doom

It isn't a happy occasion that gave me a week away from school to visit my home with my maybe-boyfriend John and my maybe-not-quite-alive-anymore best friend and roommate Mari, but I feel a burst of unmatched joy when I walk the dirt path up to my house, then drop my things and rush the rest of the way to embrace my mother the moment I see her. We crash into one another on the front steps of our house. She's in tears as we hug tightly, muttering things like, "How I've missed you," and, "My sweet, sweet Jennifer," and, "You're the light of my life."

It really takes coming home to realize how very much I miss my mother. My time at Skymark University makes me forget how comfortable and safe being back home in the countryside feels.

"John, it's a pleasure to meet you! My, my, you *are* a strapping young man," she adds as she takes a look at his brawny form, broad shoulders, and stubble dusting his handsome face. John returns her compliment with an uncharacteristic smile (the man never smiles) and says, "Now I see where Jen gets her beauty from." To that, my mother blushes bashfully and titters to herself, then says, "But not her long, winter-white hair! No one knows where she gets *that* beauty from."

And I roll my eyes and give John a *"Really?"* sort of look. He only smirks, puts an arm around me, and says, *"I love your winter-white hair,"* then gives me a little kiss.

Well, that makes one of us. This winter-white hair has given me nothing but trouble. I've been teased since I was a child. I've been unabashedly stared at in public. The Dead seem to think I'm some kind of magic millennia-old celebrity reincarnated.

I should seriously revisit my idea of dyeing it.

If only I can settle on a color.

We're guided straight through the door and into the cozy little kitchen, which overlooks the large, grassy field I used to run around in as a child with my father, lined with distant trees and a sparkling pond. The world is so vividly green out here, and the sunlight pours warmly over every inch of its beauty.

Except now, I get to enjoy the view without my dad.

My heart breaks now at the sight of it.

"You've had a long travel," notes my mother. "Come, get settled. I made you up a room, as well as the spare room for Mari. It's the same one I always set you up in when you visit," she points out to my friend Mari.

But of course, this isn't the same Mari my mother once knew. My friend is now an Undead version of herself with her same body, but it's vastly more … *quiet*. The poor girl doesn't even remember her First Life since she hasn't had a Waking Dream yet.

But I coached Mari quite a bit on the train ride over, since she must hide her Undead nature to everyone, and thus she has the graciousness to play along and say, "Of course, Mrs. Steel. Thank you. I do love that room!" Then she gives me a hopeful glance, asking with her big eyes whether she was convincing enough.

I give her a tightened smile. *I guess that'll do.*

The funeral is the very next morning. We gather on a nearby hillside with any remaining friends and family of my father's as a government official reads the words that are spoken at any person's funeral. In the center of us all is the "deceased pedestal" upon which a wooden urn is set, adorned with flowers. My father's ashes rest inside.

"They used to bury the dead," I mutter quietly to John while the official tiredly continues to recite his words. Being a studier of history, and specializing in Mythologies and the Dead, I of course know a lot on the subject. "I wonder why we don't engage in that practice anymore."

John stares darkly at the urn. "Probably because the government fears they'll come back."

Mari, with her exceptional Undead hearing, catches the words, and she turns her head to peer at the stony-eyed pair of us, anxiety tightening her face.

We share a secret now. Us three. A dark secret.

And it's a secret we have sworn to keep by signing an official government contract, each of us. The Beautiful Dead do not exist, no matter what we saw during our time in the Blight—or the Sunless Reach—or the Place

Beyond The Sun's Reach Where The Dead Live And The Living Die. It has many names, but for us, it might as well have one: The Place Where We Must Pretend We Saw Nothing, Know Nothing, And Experienced Nothing.

The shuffling of a soldier's feet draws my attention, pulling it from the official's words, and it is then that I'm reminded of the four armed guards who were sent here to ensure our safety at my father's funeral.

But I'm no fool. I know why they were *really* sent: *to ensure we do our part in keeping the Dead secret.*

Thanks for the sentiment, Skymark University.

The nighttime comes fast, but sleep doesn't come at all to me. How in the world am I supposed to enjoy and recover during my "week away from campus" with all that's gone on? A week isn't enough to put the events of the Sunless Reach behind me. I doubt a month would be enough. Or a year. Or a lifetime.

This isn't a pleasure vacation. This isn't a gift.

It's a temporary banishment while the busybodies at the university clean up our mess.

Yeah, I know better.

A knock on my half-opened bedroom door startles me. Mari stands there awkwardly, wringing her hands. *"Can I talk to you, Jen?"* she whispers.

I give a short glance at my brute boyfriend John, who had no trouble instantly falling asleep, cuddling no less than three blankets and a squishy pillow as he softly snores. I envy his mysterious ability to shut off his mind.

I rise and come with Mari out onto the porch. We occupy two creaky wicker chairs and gaze into the field.

"I ... don't feel like I belong here."

I turn to her. "Of course you belong here, Mari. What do you mean by that?"

She winces, seeming unsure how to put her feelings into words. "You're ... so kind and *patient* with me, ever since ... well, whatever happened to me." She smiles, but it falters fast. "I still feel strange. I feel ... *wrong.*"

"No, no. You're not wrong. You're ..." What do I say here? "You're fine, I'm sure of it. Just give it time."

"Time's all I have now, right? I just ..." Mari keeps wringing her hands. Her wrist is coming loose at the joint and starts to rotate in a way it shouldn't. I stare at that wrist, my stomach turning with it, as she sighs and says, "I don't think I'm happy."

Distracted by her wrist, which is now twisted a total and sickening one-hundred-and-eighty-degrees, I swallow hard and say, "I promise you'll find happiness again."

"But I—"

I grab both her hands, stopping her fretting. Her skin is colder than I expected. "I said I promise, alright? Listen to me. When you were alive—" *Oh, that's so weird to say. Too soon.* "—you were so happy. Maybe *too* happy," I tease, going for humor, despite the mixed jumble of anxiety in my chest. "You'll find that old Mari in you again. Maybe even before your Waking Dream thing, when the memory of your First Life comes back to you in an instant. Who knows. Our world is full of wonderful surprises, isn't it?"

Mari stares at our clasped hands. "Thank you, Winter. I'll just be patient and … and hope to find my happiness again. Somehow."

I smile warmly and give her hands a rub.

Until I realize what she just called me, then freeze.

Mari seems to realize it, too. "J-Jennifer, I meant." Her big, strange eyes meet mine. "Sorry. Honest mistake."

My chair creaks as I settle back into it, letting go of her hands. I stare at the dark field, lit only by the moon's pale light. With just that one word, I'm transported back to the land of the Dead.

Winter. *I've never hated a season more than I do now.*

"Jennifer? I'm sorry. I don't know why I said it."

"Maybe …" What can I possibly say? "Maybe I'm not myself either. I don't think I even shed a single tear at my father's funeral. I feel like I was … barely there. I'm barely here right now. Something in me changed over there, I think." My smile returns to me as I eye my friend. "We're both peculiar. That's why we're friends, Mari. Because we don't belong anywhere *together*."

Winter's Doom

A smile spills awkwardly from Mari's lips before she glances out at the field, then fidgets again with her fingers.

I stare down worriedly at them, hoping she doesn't accidentally pull one off.

That'd be an odd one to explain to my mother.

After Mari returns to her room (to sit on the bed and just stare at a wall, I suppose, as the Dead don't have any need for sleep) I return to mine, but can't go back to sleep. I sit at my desk instead, then pull out that dull rock and stare at it again. I study it with the precision of a tired scientist burning the midnight oil, curious what secrets it holds within.

Why am I so obsessed?

Maybe a part of me was left over there, a part of me I don't understand. Maybe the reason Mari's words bother me is because I never felt I belonged anywhere, either.

And holding this stone—this strange, unknowable stone—makes me feel a little less alone with my secret … almost like the stone is my friend.

Even if it still feels like it's watching me, waiting for something.

Strange, I know. Maybe even a little lunatic. But after my venture to the land of the Dead and back, I'm willing to believe in just about anything.

Even walking, talking Undead people.

And the Whispers.

"Do you remember that day in the gardens," I say quietly to John's gently snoring form, "when you stole this black rock from its glass casing, and in our escape, I dropped it on the ground? I watched flowers wilt before my eyes as I picked it back up, as if the rock itself somehow … *drank* the very life from them."

John doesn't respond. He's lost in a sea of dreams.

Anima … Is that what this stone is? Or is that a power that lives within the stone? Or a force that it gathers? Or some kind of Undead energy that it awakens? The studies all contradict one another, so I can't rely on the books from the official libraries to answer my questions.

I need something … *more.*

"Goodnight, John." I pocket the stone again, then take my place back in bed next to him and stare at the ceiling for another hour in thought before at last drifting off.

The rest of the week speeds by faster than I want it to. I always seem to wake up earlier than John, despite my trouble sleeping, which means I get to spend a lot of time with my mother each morning. She asks a thousand and one questions about John, of course, teasing me about how *handsome* and *hunky* and *"strong silent type"* she thinks he is. I have to laugh and blush and roll my eyes with a smile on my face, making my mother press me more for details about him. It's all I can do to feel normal again, even if just for a fleeting second.

Winter's Doom

"I'm so sorry I wasn't here," I suddenly catch myself saying.

My mother, in the middle of sipping her coffee, stops.

"I should have been here. When Dad died. I should have been here and not left you alone."

Her forehead creases. "But you didn't have a choice. You were stolen away by that crazy Diviner. A hostage to a crazy woman."

I avert my gaze.

The contract we all signed even requires me to lie to my own mother about the truth. To everyone I know and love. Maybe even someday to myself.

"What was it like?"

I flinch and stare at her. "What?"

"Over there. The Blight. The Other Side." Her voice is faint, faraway. "Did you see anything? Did you ... Did you experience something strange, Jennifer? You can tell me."

My throat tightens right up. I glance back at the front door for some reason, perhaps giving a moment's thought to those *guard goons* the government sent to watch over my father's funeral.

They're still there, by the way. Only now, they stand guard at the end of my mother's driveway.

I'll be watched by the government until the day *I* die.

I return my gaze to my mother. "The Blight ... is in desperate need of your skillful gardening hands, for sure."

The pair of us share a smile.

Not another word is uttered about the matter.

When it's at last the time for us to return to campus, my mother pulls me aside while John and Mari gather their things. "Sweetheart, I've been meaning to give you this." She hands me a small package wrapped in a soft brown paper and tied with a string, as if it's a parcel of delicate foodstuffs from the market. It's heavier than I expect. "It's from your father."

My eyes flash. "Dad?" I glance down at it. "What is it?"

"Keep it hidden, alright? It's best if you look at it in private, I think. Your father left it to you."

"Why did you wait until I'm leaving to give me this? What is it? Why won't you tell me?"

"Please don't open it until you return to campus. That may be best. There are too many ..." She glances at the door herself. *What is going on?* "Too many eyes, I think. Yes, far too many eyes." She presses the package to my chest with a hand. "Stow it away in your things. Your father wanted you to have it. Please." She hugs me at once, squeezing me so tightly, I could break. "Just take it and don't say goodbye, alright? I'd keep you here another week if I could. A month or two. I hate that you have to go back to that school."

I close my eyes. "I love you, Mom."

"I love you more."

Winter's Doom

The weight of the package somehow makes my entire bag ten times heavier than it ought to be. I know it's my imagination, but even as we walk the long dirt road to the train, I feel like I'm dragging with me a great big weight.

Unlike the ride here, John and I get seats next to each other while Mari sits two rows ahead, still fidgeting and wringing her hands. It's against John's big shoulder that I tiredly lean my head, hugging my whole bag to my chest. I'm clearly unable to part with it even for the journey back to campus.

"Jen? Did you hear me?"

I lift my head from his shoulder. "What?"

"I said I've been reading this week." John nods at the overhead carriage where his own bag sits. "Those books on engineering you borrowed from the library for me."

"Oh. Good." I offer a distracted smile. "Better to be prepared before next term starts and you're a *real* student at the university."

"Are you alright?"

In natural Jennifer Steel fashion, I deflect his question with one of my own. "Did you learn anything interesting in those books of yours?"

John studies my face for a second before answering. "I read a chapter on the strength of different forms of matter and types of materials. Oh, and I read a whole thing about how hovercrafts work, which is pretty advanced stuff."

"Sounds like you skipped around in the book," I tease, then give a glance at my bag, my curiosity nagging me.

"Also read a bit about explosives. Did you know our military used to make secret bombs disguised as those cube-shaped metal pods that food is normally transferred in? You can identify them by the yellow—"

"Okay, sorry, I can't wait anymore." I yank open my bag and rummage inside.

John, interrupted abruptly by my outburst, watches me with confusion as I pull out the package my father left to me. After a moment's reluctance, I undo the string and let the paper fall away, revealing its contents.

Three small books in a stack, worn and leathery.

"*Diary of the*—?" reads John in a hush, stopping before uttering the last word.

"Dead," I finish anyway.

John stares at me harshly. "*What is this?*" he whispers. "*Why do you have these books?*"

"My father left them to me in his will. He wanted me to have them for … for some unknown reason. But … I've read these before. All three of them. It's a series. Why would my father …?" Then I notice the author's name. "Megan? That's not who wrote these. It's supposed to be Doctor Ardor Timewise, a renowned archaeologist and professor. Unless it's a coincidence, and this is merely a different series with the same title." I flip the book over, then glance at the other two. "But that seems even less likely, considering the oddly specific subject matter. Who is this 'Megan' …?"

"Jen, I don't care who that is, or why he gave them to you," whispers John, growing agitated. *"You can't have those. You need to put them away before someone—"*

I turn my face to John's. "These had belonged to my father. There's an important reason he gave them to me."

"That may very well be," John hisses, his eyes darting around us, as if all the other passengers on the train are listening to our every breath, *"but I doubt he anticipated the situation you'd be in, and how dangerous it is to have books like that in your possession. We can't easily keep our end of the bargain if we're still showing so much interest in the Dead."*

"The author's name is different. 'Megan'. Who is …" I squint at the book, then open it, glancing at the first page with equal parts curiosity—and mounting frustration. "No last name? Just 'Megan'? I can't even look her up in a database without a last name. There must be a hundred *Megans* in our Jurisdiction alone. Who the hell is she?"

"It's way too risky. Put those books away. Or better yet, leave them behind entirely."

My eyes turn harsh when I look on him again. "This is all I have left of my father, John. I might have to keep my mouth shut about the truth for the rest of my life, but I won't discard my father's last gift to me."

John's face is stone and fury as we lock eyes, each of us more stubborn than the other.

Until finally I take a breath, close my eyes, then allow caution to override my impenetrable, oftentimes reckless zeal. It's gotten us into too much trouble as it is, to be fair. "Okay. I'll put them away."

John nods. "Good."

And just like that, peace is restored.

The peace is short-lived. When we at last arrive at campus, the first thing we hear is chanting and yelling. John and I share a look, then rise from our seats and, along with other passengers, rush to the windows on the other side of the train to look for the commotion.

Posters are spread all over the walls: *THE DEAD LIVE. WE HAVE BEEN LIED TO. BELIEVE IN THE DEAD.* Groups of angry students march the campus streets, chanting and holding signs. All of Skymark University has exploded into madness, mayhem, and riots of protest.

So much for keeping our secret.

Chapter Two

A Grim Welcoming

Our bags still in hand, John, Mari, and I attempt to cross the campus amidst the protests and chaos, but our movement is slowed by gathering crowds and marching groups of sign-wielding students.

At this time of day, classes should be in session, but even the professors are standing outside their buildings, worry and wonder in their eyes, some of them aghast at what they're witnessing of their students. Authorities are spread out everywhere attempting to bring to order any of the students, but they are yet far too outnumbered.

"What's going on?" I ask a nearby student—a young woman who I swear I might have taken a grammar class with one semester.

Regardless, she doesn't recognize me, too caught up in the excitement of everything around her. "President Vale and the government are full of lies! The Dead live!" she cries out, barely giving me a moment of her attention as she slaps another poster to the wall and scurries off.

John looks at me. "This isn't good."

"No," I agree. "It isn't."

We're just a mere courtyard away from our campus condominium when we find the largest gathering of all: a vast group of students huddled around the fountain, upon the stone lip of which stands a familiar, pale-faced poet, who is addressing the crowd with an impassioned speech.

"Do you remember the spark of curiosity that lived in your hearts when you first became a Skymark enrollee?" the poet asks of the crowd, inspired. "The spark lived in all of us. But I've never known a spark stronger than the one that lives in Jennifer Steel: the one who is being silenced by our school."

I stop at those words, standing at the back of the crowd.

"What is a university now," he asks, "but a vessel of what the government wants us to know? What is real knowledge nowadays, except an edited version of the truth? Are we not owed the truth, or are our minds seen as too gentle to handle it?"

Then his eyes find mine in the crowd.

I freeze underneath them, terrified I've been spotted.

The poet smiles. "I believe in Jennifer Steel," he then says, his soft gaze upon me. "The real knowledge we seek is out there. This university can no longer be relied on. Believe in the Beautiful Dead!"

Winter's Doom

From the side, authorities are pushing through the crowd, fighting their way toward the center where the fountain is.

"And in honor of the Dead," he says to the crowd, his time ticking away as the authorities slowly close in upon him, "I renounce my given human name. From now on, I'll encompass the very Undeath our university tries to hide from us. From now on, I am the Grim Reaper made human!" His eyes meet mine once more, and they are alight with brilliance. "I'll only answer to the name *Grim!*"

Then the poet is swiped off the rim of the fountain upon which he stood, and after a splash of water from the armored men and women, the poet is dragged away, and the crowd erupts into chanting his name.

And it's right past me that he is roughly dragged along by the authorities, who hold a firm grip on either of his arms. "Your legacy will live on," he promises me as he passes by, out of breath. "I believe in the Dead, Jennifer! I will keep the Dead alive!"

I really wish he wouldn't.

Two minutes later, we push through the door of our condominium and let it shut heavily at our backs. The three of us collapse on the couch in the living room—our bags discarded and forgotten on the floor—as we stare through the floor-to-ceiling glass windows, observing with anxious eyes the chaos of our campus beyond.

"What is happening?" I ask rhetorically, numb.

John cradles his head between his knees, overcome. "This isn't good. This isn't good at all."

"What is happening?" I can't stop asking the question. I'm losing my mind. "We left the campus just a week ago. Everything was peaceful. Everything was in order. Now the school is flipped upside-down. What is happening?"

"We'll figure this out," says John, suddenly wrapping me in his arms and holding me against his chest on the couch. "Don't worry. I've got you. We're safe."

I'm trembling.

And I hardly feel safe at all.

Especially not while listening to the click-click-click of Mari incessantly rotating her wrist around and around—her new favorite anxious habit.

We eat something out of the fridge, not daring to see if the dormitory cafeterias are operating amidst the riots and uprising. I'm not hungry, so I don't touch a speck of John's mixed greens and meat. Mari doesn't eat anymore, so she just sits glumly in her room—and even from there I can hear the *click-click-click*. What is that unsettling sound, anyway? Is it her bones snapping? Is it tendons twisting around every time she rotates her wrist? I can't stand it and I don't even know what it is.

"The crowds are dissipating," John notes a few hours later while the sun gently sets on the other side of the tall buildings, beams of its glorious light peeking out between them. "Maybe this was some organized protest day, and it's all over with now."

It'll never be over, that much I know. But I can't bear to give John a response—whether a harshly truthful one or a pacifying lie—so I just keep silent as I flip pages in this version of *Diary of the Dead* by Megan. It's been a while since I read the first version, so I'm struggling to discern the differences.

"So what's that about, exactly?" asks John from the window at which he stands, leaning against the glass with his arms folded.

He's finally taken note of what I'm reading, curled up on the far end of the couch as I am. "It's a fictional story about a girl's journey in a land that's been taken over by the Undead. But the story is riddled with facts about them and has been looked at as less of a fictional tale and more of someone's actual account." I bite my lip and shake my head. "It's all the same, just the same as the archaeologist Ardor's version, from what I remember."

"Do you think he stole her work?"

I look up from the pages. "Who?"

"This Megan person. Do you think she's the real author of the book?" John shrugs and glances back out the window, the sunset painting his face a deep golden color. "I wouldn't be surprised if she's the girl the whole book is actually about. Maybe it's her own account of her life, and some rich and powerful professor stole it and claimed it as his own fictional spin on the Undead."

"I don't know." I return my eyes to the book, finishing the paragraph I was reading, then flipping the page. My hand, whether by habit or just to ensure it's still there, slides into my pocket where a certain rock still sits. I play with it, turning it around and around with my fingers, fidgeting as I continue to read.

John sighs and pushes away from the window. "I need a shower." And with a soft closing of my bedroom door, he's gone.

Alone now in the living room, I pull the stone out of my pocket and take to staring into it again like a crystal ball full of answers—my latest weirdo obsession, clearly.

I just can't seem to separate myself from it, bothered by something.

And I don't know what that something is.

So in lieu of trying to figure out said something, I put myself into the words of the books my father left me. I don't know why, but I'm determined to find some hidden meaning in them, something he intended me to find, a message, a clue, a discovery—anything.

It's strange that he'd leave me something like this to begin with. He never thought highly of my choice in studies—or at least that's the impression I got.

Winter's Doom

What if I was wrong this whole time?

What if my father was as obsessed with discovering the truth about the Dead as I am?

I read a chapter about the girl and the rules her camp abided by. I read about her brother and the day he went missing. *Yes, yes, I've read all of this before.* I skip several chapters, skimming for something new, and reach the part of the story where, for twelve long years, the girl grew into a woman, lived peacefully among the Dead as their mayor of sorts, and watched the world slowly turn from dead to alive. *"It comes in cycles,"* the narrator says. *"Life, Death, Life, Death, then Life again."*

My fidgeting with the stone stops at once.

I look at it, reminded of something.

My time in the Whispers.

And the Dead I named Corpsey who was with me that day.

What became of him? Is he still wandering about in that godforsaken place, searching for blood, for answers, for a purpose? Does he wonder as much as I do about what the Whispers told us that day?

The two children with green eyes, the two young men with yellow eyes, and the old wise man and woman who glowed as white as the nighttime stars. *It comes in cycles ... Life, Death, Life ...*

My eyes return to the page, and I catch the last words of a paragraph: *"... until I see my friend Winter again."*

I blink.

I rub my eyes, lean forward, and reread the words.

Winter? I've never heard mention of a Winter in the first version. "My friend Winter" …?

There is a booming knock at the door.

I jump in place and slap a hand to my chest, my heart racing. The book drops to the floor, closing itself. I look over my shoulder at the door while squeezing the stone in my sweaty palm, terrified.

I wait.

Boom, boom, boom of a fist against the door. "Jennifer Steel. John Mason. Marianne Gable," comes a stern voice from the other side.

I'm trembling again. I can't seem to bring myself to move.

My bedroom door flies open and John emerges at once, alarmed. He wears just a towel around his waist, his muscled chest gleaming with water from his shower and his short hair matted and wet.

His eyes meet mine, alarmed.

I hold my breath. Should we answer the door? Should we pretend we're not here? Should we—?

"Jennifer Steel. John Mason. Marianne Gable. This is the authority," they announce almost tiredly, as if they've made the same call to twenty other houses. "I remind you that you are required by law to answer your door."

Winter's Doom

John and I both seem to make the same decision at once, as if our minds are linked. I rise from the couch and kick the book underneath it, then pocket my stone. John rushes back into the bedroom to throw on pants and a shirt, which sticks to his wet form, before hiding the other two books in a drawer. Together now, the pair of us head for the door. Mari stands at her bedroom door, having emerged herself, and watches us with wide eyes.

"Jennifer Steel. John Mason. Marianne—"

I pull open the door.

No less than five faces of armored authorities meet mine.

"Yes?" I greet them, unsettled.

It's the one in front who addresses us, a woman with a cold, brusque voice and dark eyes. "The three of you are being summoned for an audience with President Vale of Skymark University. Bring only yourselves and nothing else. We will escort you, and we depart now."

I glance at John. His jaw is set tight, causing his whole face to tense, water still dripping from his hair.

"What are we being taken to President Vale for?" I ask the woman, feeling indignant. "We only just returned to campus. We had nothing in the least to do with the riots or protests, and we're—"

"Come with us, Ms. Steel, Mr. Mason, and Ms. Gable. No harm will come to you if you cooperate."

"I *am* cooperating. That's what I'm trying to tell you."

"Jen," murmurs John warningly. "Let's just go with them and not cause any trouble. I'm sure it's something they just want cleared up, or possibly could be something unrelated to the riots entirely."

I'm not so easily convinced.

"Jennifer?" comes Mari's tiny voice from behind.

I turn. Her round face and dopey eyes meet mine, and for this one moment, I truly see someone who is lost in our world, floating along, pulled by the consequences of everyone else's actions but her own. I can't even begin to imagine what poor Mari is going through, her existence literally dragged along on the whim of whatever happens to me. She didn't ask for this life.

She didn't ask for her Unlife either.

I reach out and give her hand a squeeze. "It'll all be alright, Mari." I turn to face the authorities. "We will go."

"It wasn't a request, but an order," states the woman matter-of-factly. "Come now."

And like that, the three of us are escorted down the steps of our condominium under the waning daylight and into the mouth of a small vehicle, which swiftly carries us around the familiar street that wraps around the outskirts of the campus.

Sitting in the middle, I take hold of John's hand on one side and Mari's on the other. Then, in silence, the three of

Winter's Doom

us stare out the window of the vehicle and watch the buildings fly past our eyes, with no idea of what's to come. My heart thumps in my chest so uncomfortably, I feel like I could faint. It wasn't long ago that I spoke with the coolly polite yet offputting President Vale, who insisted I called her Rosella. She presented herself as a friend in whom I could confide, despite being the head of the university. She had us sign statements to deny all that we saw and experienced in the Blight. She smiled warmly at me and was quick to assure me all would be alright.

I feel as if her assurance is already fast fading.

"I shouldn't have stuck the knife in my head," says Mari suddenly.

I turn to her. "What?"

"The knife. During your presentation to the school. I shouldn't ... I really shouldn't have done that, proving to everyone about the Beautiful Dead. I'm the reason all of this is happening."

"No, Mari, no, no. That isn't ..." I squeeze her hand and swallow down my doubts. *She might be right. If she hadn't done that, then none of this ...* "That isn't true, Mari. Don't blame ..." *What if Mari is entirely to blame? What if she's right?* "Don't blame yourself for what's happening."

"But it's my fault."

I turn to John for help, but he's looking away, his jaw tensed again. His eyes are so dark with thoughts, I can barely look into them without feeling the fear and anxiety surging within his chest.

This isn't Mari's fault. This is mine. I'm the whole reason her heart no longer beats.

Suddenly, I decide not to say anything at all, stare straight ahead, and keep gripping Mari's hand.

The vehicle comes to such an abrupt stop, all three of us lurch forward. The doors open, and we're brought up a long flight of stone steps that lead to the doors of the intimidatingly tall administrative building. Once inside, we're ushered through a heated crowd of upset adults— parents of the protesters who were arrested today, perhaps?—and after a code is inputted into a panel on the wall, we're taken up an elevator directly to the top floor.

When the great doors of President Vale's office open, I feel a wash of dread run over me. We'd only been here just a week ago. It's far too soon to be back. Across the daunting length of the room, President Vale stands before us at her long, long desk that stretches nearly wall-to-wall. She wears an off-white neck-to-toe pantsuit with a vivid, emerald green scarf thrown about her neck.

But unlike the first time we visited, she is not alone at that desk. On either side of her sits a few other officials in dark suits, and behind them, armored guards much like the ones who went to my countryside home with me "for my own protection" stand at attention.

Winter's Doom

"Jennifer. John. Marianne," President Vale greets us coolly, her voice echoing and godlike. "Have a seat."

After a glance at one another, John, Mari, and I cross the room and sit in three chairs that await us in front of her staggeringly wide desk.

It's in approaching that I realize one of the men sitting at her desk is Professor Praun, my cool-mannered, somewhat intimidating, hard-eyed history professor, who happens to share knowledge of the Undead truth, yet took part in ensuring I keep said truth buried. His choice in partaking of the odd trend of shaving ones' eyebrows off gives his deep umber skin an oddly plastic texture, even with his pristinely-trimmed dark goatee. The man looks as if he could sit still for a whole hour without so much as a twitch of his papery eyelids—a perfect mannequin.

He had spoken against me focusing my work on the Beautiful Dead and chided me after Mari's big act during my presentation. *I don't suspect he's my biggest fan.*

"Sit," states President Vale once more.

We sit. The chairs are cold despite the padding.

President Vale does not sit. Behind the woman stands a window so tall, it towers over us three times any of our heights. Her round, plain, featureless face has no sign of warmth today, even with the few visible freckles on her cheeks, and her wavy shoulder-length ruby-red hair seems a tone duller than I remember.

Daryl Banner

I can't stand the discomfort. "Why are we here?" I blurt at once, unable to contain myself. Why practice caution? Judging by the people here, we're all in on the secret of the Dead. "We've done nothing wrong. We've honored your deal."

"Jen …" murmurs John warningly.

President Vale gives me a blank, curious look before she speaks. "I am sure you have no doubt seen the state of Skymark University since your trip home last week."

"I didn't just 'take a trip home'," I retort carelessly. "I was paying respects to my *dead father*."

"My condolences."

Her "condolences" ring hollow in my ears. "And yes, we've seen the campus. Everyone's lost their minds."

"Riots. Protesting. Vandalism. Six injured professors. Two librarians cornered by a crowd of angry students. It is the biggest uproar our jurisdiction has had in over forty-five years, big enough to involve the government—and *three* local authority centers—to regain order here."

"But what do we have to do with it?" I ask agitatedly. John whispers my name again and reaches for my hand, but I yank it away, my temper flared. "We weren't even here. We were hours away."

"I am joined today with others who, like you, are aware of the goings-on across the sea," continues the president in her frustratingly calm tone of voice. "Some of

34

my colleagues here work for the government. Some of them are employed here at the school, like your professor of history here: Professor Praun. Some, both. They bore witness to your presentation a week ago, and they know of the statement all four of you signed."

Four ...?

Then, as if having forgotten his existence entirely, I remember the fourth member of our rescued party at once. The delivery boy, Connor Easton, who was brought along for the journey against his will. The blue-eyed, youthful blond was in the back of the hovercraft we stole, unbeknownst to us. It was his very first day on the job. He was not happy to join us.

I'm not sure I can count him as a friend in all of this.

But there was a fifth among us, too: Dana the Diviner. And the statements we signed were to corroborate a lie: that Dana, in a crazed and delusional state, took hostage of us, stole a hovercraft, and flew us to the land of the Dead. Dana was blamed for everything so as to absolve us survivors of any potential charges.

With Dana having voluntarily chosen to remain in the Blight when we were rescued, there would be no way for the public to verify the truth.

Dana was our unknowing scapegoat.

"Yes, we did sign statements," I agree firmly, "and you are just as much bound to the terms of them as I am."

"However, they were signed under a very specific set of circumstances." The president spreads her hands. "And the circumstances have sadly changed."

The words draw my blood cold.

The circumstances have sadly changed …

"President …" I start.

"My colleagues and I have discussed this extensively. We now have new orders from the government regarding how to proceed. Your previous statements, I'm afraid, are now considered legally null and void."

I rise from my chair at once. "What?? That's absurd! You can't do that!"

My simple action caused the guards to stir from their statuesque positions. But they are frozen once again by a curt lift of the president's hand, stopping them. "Ms. Steel, please remain calm. No harm will come to you or your friends by my hand, this I promise you. What we're about to engage in is simply a matter of … oh, how should I put it? … bureaucracy and formalism, to satisfy an ever-needy government. They want answers. We want funding. This is how things are done in order to get things done."

I furrow my brow. "But what does that mean for us?"

"It is simple. The three of you will be taken from here to a government facility where there will be a trial before a Judge Supreme. I assure you, it is merely a formality. You will answer questions according to the truth—*but omitting your knowledge of the Dead, of course, of which we will never again speak."*

"A trial?" I turn to John, then Mari. My own confusion is mirrored in their eyes. "How can you possibly assure me that it's just a ... a ... a 'formality', this trial? It sounds really serious."

"It is, but only on paper. What I need—and expect—from the three of you as Skymark students, is to behave with professionalism, to answer the Judge's questions dutifully, and to represent the university in the best of lights. Then when all is finished, you will return here just in time for your classes. Do I have your understanding?" She glances from me, to John, to ever-clueless Mari.

I feel every bit of misgiving a person can feel, yet I swallow down my anxieties and give her a simple, "Yes, ma'am, President Rosella Vale."

"Ah, you remembered to call me by my name." The president smiles warmly, then turns her eyes onto John. "And your understanding, John Mason?"

He glances quickly at me before giving the president a nod himself. "Yeah."

And finally she looks upon Mari. "And yours?"

Mari helplessly wrings her hands as she stares at the president, unblinking, unbreathing, uneverything. "Yes," she recites robotically.

"Good." The president nods to someone behind us.

Guards come to my side and take hold of my arms. Startled by their presence, I struggle against them for all of two seconds before realizing they're simply performing a duty. With the forceful way in which they're holding me, I can barely manage a glance over my shoulder to look at John, who is being less-than-gently ushered off by a pair of his own guards, who look twice the size of mine. "John?" I call out over my shoulder, worry bubbling up inside my chest despite all the president's assurances. "Jen, I'll see you soon," he shouts back, his voice breaking despite trying to sound brave. "Be strong. Just do what they say. Don't let anyone or anything get to you."

Outside the room, I'm guided down one hall while John is taken down another. "Wait, why aren't we—? John!" I call out again, but the guards ignore me, and when we turn a corner, I lose sight of the only two people in the world I care about right now. "John!" I call out feebly, despite everything. "John, be strong, too! John!"

But there's no response, and it's no use. The three of us are separated now, pulled apart like appendages off a helpless Dead, like fragile legs off a spider, like leaves off a tree in preparation for a cold and terrible winter.

Chapter Three

The Trial

Well, this isn't exactly how I planned to spend my Friday evening.

Or maybe it's Saturday already.

The walls of the cell I'm placed in are the ever inviting color of dead flesh—grey, bare, smooth, some polished kind of metal that's cold to the touch and oddly clammy in spots. There's a small bed with a stiff mattress on one side and a metal toilet on the other. There aren't any windows, so my only source of light is a thin fluorescent strip that lines the whole room halfway up the wall.

But let's look on the bright side: my new temporary home is remarkably clean. Not a speck of scum or dirt anywhere, in fact. Not even on the floor around the cold, unwelcoming toilet, where I expected at least a courtesy puddle of someone else's urine. I mean, someone should really commend the janitorial staff who are employed at this pristine, government-grade prison facility. Those men and women clearly work overtime.

Also, there's no annoying guards ghoulishly staring at me from a distance for the first time in a week.

That thought is the most comforting, I find.

I sit in the corner of the cell, hug my knees to my chest, and think of the one thing that doesn't comfort me at all: the thought of what is to come of John and Mari, my friends who both advised against me journeying to the Sunless Reach. If I had listened to them back then, we'd be relaxing at the peaceful, riot-free Skymark University right now, attending our classes without a worry in the world, and blissfully unaware of the Dead.

I was made to change into a simple set of grey linen pants and a shirt, too. Prison formalities or something.

Grey is not my color.

Unfortunately, that also means they took from me my only possession: the black stone John and I took from the gardens long ago, as it was stuffed away in my pocket.

In other words: a rock that wasn't mine to begin with.

Is it strange that I miss *it*, most of all?

That's not the only troubling thought I've had while sitting here in my cell awaiting the trial. Despite President Vale's assurances, I imagine the authorities will likely raid our condominium. That means my father's books will be found, as lazily as we hid them, and they'll probably be burned. His last dear gift to me will be seen as offensive icons of blasphemy. Hell, maybe they'll even consider the possession of those books yet one more offense to pin on me during this "formality" of a trial the president insisted we be put through. And if I'm lucky, I'll be released from this place just in time for my one hundredth birthday.

Can we just get this over with?

The sound of footsteps touch my ear. I look up just as the metal door to my cell swings open with a screechy groan, and a man steps inside. The door is shut and locked with a *clang*, and the man peers down at me.

Professor Praun.

I rise to my feet at once. "Professor?"

He stays right where he is. "I warned you, Ms. Steel."

Well, that's a lovely greeting. "Professor, I know this whole trial thing is some kind of official government business, or whatever the president said, but we haven't even been here on campus to incite any riots. Why do—?"

"I meant before you even left to visit the Blight in the first place, Ms. Steel." His eyes turn hard. "In my office, the day you chose to steal a hovercraft and head for the Blight, I had warned you. I attempted to strongly dissuade you against pursuing your studies. I warned you loud and clear, and yet you defied me still, did you not?"

"Well, yes. But—"

"And after studying the Dead extensively, you found a truth buried in the books you couldn't ignore, and you chased that truth across the ocean where you came face to face with those who had lungs that don't breathe, hearts that don't beat, and stomachs that yearned desperately for your blood. Confirm that it is so."

I give him a look. "President Vale wants me to deny their existence to the Judge."

"I am not the Judge. Confirm that what I said is true."

I sigh. "Alright. Yes, it is so."

He reaches toward me suddenly, startling me, and before I realize what he's meaning to do, his hand slips into my pocket.

Something small yet heavy drops into it.

I lift an eyebrow, confused.

Professor Praun's eyes narrow as he retracts his hand, then his voice lowers. "Good." His demeanor changes at once. "Because it is of absolute importance that you keep your truths straight, the real one *and* the false one. Your life may depend on the distinction between the two."

Wait, what? "S-Sir?"

"I am speaking to you off the record," he goes on, and his words are uncharacteristically rushed, as if he's pressed for time. "They do not know I am here. You are going to attend the trial soon. But should the Judge Supreme not lean in your favor, the real trial you will face awaits you across the sea, in the land beyond the sun's reach where the Dead live and the Living die. Are you paying attention to my words, Jennifer?"

Winter's Doom

Jennifer. He never calls me by my first name. "I—I'm—P-Professor, you're going too fast. I thought the trial was just a government formality?"

"Have you learned nothing? Listen to me." He grabs hold of my wrists and brings his face alarmingly close to mine, and his voice lowers to near nothing. "When you reunite with the Queen of them all," he tells me with great severity, "you must give her a message. Tell her: *'The Green Eye opens when the Yellow closes. The White has arrived.'* Tell her those exact words, Jennifer."

His breath smells faintly of blood. Why does it smell faintly of blood? "Professor, you're scaring me."

"Repeat them back to me. The words. Quickly."

I sputter three times before managing to recite them. "The Green opens when the Yellow closes. The White—"

"The Green *Eye. Eye*, Jennifer."

"The Green … *Eye* … opens when the Yellow closes. The White has arrived."

He straightens his back, seeming satisfied. "Good." Then he nods toward my pocket. "Keep it safe."

And with that, the man abruptly turns, pulls open the door, and lets himself out as fast as he had come in. The metal door shuts heavily, and I'm left standing there with my lips parted, baffled beyond words.

The Green Eye opens …? What was that about?

Tell the Queen of them all? Who in the heck is that?

I reach into my pocket, bewildered, and pull out the gift he dropped into it.

The black stone.

He must have had access to the belongings of the people being held here, apparently, or was somehow able to gain access to mine. But why this stone? How did he know I had it in the first place, and why would he go through so much trouble to get it back to me?

After some time passes, I reclaim my little seat in the corner of my cell, and ruminate over his stern words of warning for a long, troubling while, fidgeting with the stone in my hand.

President Vale said no harm would come to us.

She swore it. She swore to each of us, to our faces.

There were even government officials there with her. She wouldn't lie to us with them as witnesses, right?

I pour my worries into the stone. "No matter what happens, at least you and I are back together." I feel strangely accompanied—and also a bit silly for talking to a rock. "You came along with me for my dad's funeral, too. You're always there when I need you."

Maybe I think I see my father deep within the stone.

Maybe he's not really gone.

I wonder if John is sitting in a cell somewhere else in this vast prison, staring at the smooth metal walls.

And hating me.

Winter's Doom

Hating me for putting him in this position. Hating me for taking his future the day we met. Hating me for giving him that ticket to the garden where we committed our first crime—a crime no one's yet charging us with—of stealing the very rock that sits in my palm.

Maybe all of this is the rock's fault.

A noisy rattling at my door makes me jump. I pocket the stone just as my door swings back open with a creaky groan. I'm greeted by two tall guards in full armor, their faces covered by big metal helmets. "This way, Ms. Steel."

Guess it's time to get this trial thing over with.

I pay little attention to where I'm being taken, just putting one foot in front of the other as the guards dutifully guide me down a complicated web of dark passageways that all look the same to me. And in a matter of minutes, I'm brought before another set of metal doors, but these ones are considerably larger than any I've seen before.

When they open, I'm awestruck.

Before me is a room so huge, it might span the width and length of ten courtyards. Its walls are blinding white from the stark and powerful lighting, and the ceiling is made of a domed glass, giving a view of the dark night sky peppered with stars. A long aisle, sandwiched by rows upon rows of benches—at which only a few people sit here and there—leads to a podium where I am led.

Stopping at it, then let go by the guards to stand there alone, I feel as if I've been dropped off at the bottom of a vast, white ocean, the walls miles and miles away, the top of the water so high, it kisses the moon.

Seated far ahead of (and above) me is a woman at a podium of her own—a Judge Supreme. I can't pick out any distinguishable features across the distance other than she looks old and her hair is grey and curly, but I don't need to be up close to know she isn't a woman I should humor in any way. She wears a judge's blue gown with the strange white, square-shaped hat that is customary of higher-ranked Judges.

"Jennifer Steel," comes her voice, booming across the room (or should I say sports stadium?) as if projected by a microphone. On second thought, considering the vast size of the space, it would make perfect sense that she has one.

"Judge," I address her, then blink with astonishment at the volume of my own voice, projected by *my* podium. "Wow, goodness, this is loud," I continue to mutter, like a total idiot. And my echo answers back: *This is loud, this is loud, this is loud …*

The Judge carries on as if I never spoke. "You stand before Judge Enea, Supreme of Jurisdiction 10 through 12, charged with the crimes of human abduction, stealing and damaging property belonging to Skymark University, and disruptive Undead mongering."

Winter's Doom

Undead mongering. Well, that's certainly a way to put it. "Judge Supreme, may I clarify that I—"

"No word is needed from the accused," she states plainly, cutting me off. "You will be able to speak in your defense after testimony. The court will now acknowledge our first and only witness to the accused: Connor Easton."

I freeze to the spot.

East?

Another podium I hadn't noticed off some distance to my left is at once occupied by the young, rosy face of Connor Easton, the delivery boy who unwittingly joined us for our adventure. He is so far away that for a moment I think his hair has turned as white as mine, until I realize he's dressed formally in his delivery boy uniform with his white cap on top, covering his bright blond strands.

"So tell us," the Judge begins. "What happened on the date of the hovercraft abduction?"

Connor doesn't look my way when he speaks. "I was carrying out a delivery on my first day of employment, a delivery of foodstuffs to the Skymark University facilities. The accused, Jennifer Steel, took the hovercraft while I was occupied in one of its closets. I begged her several times to let me off the stolen hovercraft, but my requests were repeatedly denied. She was with John Mason and her roommate Marianne. My life was irresponsibly put in danger by the accused. I am lucky to be alive."

I swallow hard. This "trial" is feeling a lot more like a real trial than President Vale let on. "Connor ..." I try.

"For the benefit of this Court," announces the Judge, ignoring me outright, "please point to and identify the so-named abductor of whom you speak."

Connor's eyes finally meet mine—tiny and far away—and with a single certain finger, he points in my direction.

I grip my podium, causing a reverberant *thump* to cast out across the space—*Thump, thump, thump* ... "You know I had no choice, East. We were all already long off the ground when I even noticed you were aboard the hovercraft with us. I wouldn't have willingly—"

"There will be no commentary from the accused until the testimony—" the Judge starts to repeat.

"—put you in any danger," I stubbornly persist. "You and I became friends over there, East. Companions! We all looked out for each other. You and I—"

Before the Judge can speak, Connor suddenly has more to say, and it all comes out in a furious fit of rage—directed straight at me: "I could have *died* over there! I didn't want to see what I saw. Don't you know I've had nightmares every night since I've been home?? I keep thinking I'm still over there. I keep seeing them coming for my face, coming to tear off my flesh, coming to—"

"And what was it, exactly, that you saw?" asks Judge Enea in a clipped tone.

48

Winter's Doom

The cold question sends a ringing, deathly silence across the entire auditorium. Not a muscle moves. Not a breath is taken.

Connor's eyes flash wide, as if terror has suddenly gripped him around the throat with an ice-cold hand.

I stare at him, wide-eyed.

Did he just go too far?

Was he not supposed to say any of that?

Something awful, dark, and sickly crosses the boy's face as he wrestles with his words. Then, as if a robot has been implanted in his brain, Connor faces Judge Enea and dutifully states: "I saw a lot of dead trees, wastelands, and nothing else, your Honor Supreme."

"Oh?" She crosses her bony arms and smirks at him. "So what is this of 'them' coming for your face, or coming to tear off your … 'flesh' …? Is that what you said?"

Connor shivers, swallows, then blurts, "N-No one."

"Can you please clarify for the Court? Be specific."

"No one and nothing. I meant the nightmares. I have nightmares. The *nightmares* come clawing for my face. Nothing real. We saw nothing over there. There is no such thing as the Living Dead. No such thing at all. It is all folklore and make-believe and nothing."

My jaw drops.

He's been coached. Or threatened.

He's to deny the existence of the Dead entirely.

Maybe his deal with President Vale was the only one that was *not* nullified between the four of us.

I face the Judge now, taking a new tack entirely. "It's true," I state at once. "He is right. I've done all the things he's stated. Connor Easton is blameless. And while he may have greatly aided in our survival across the narrow ocean, he would not have had to, had my recklessness not brought him with us in the first place. Connor is a good, honest person, and did not deserve what troubles came to him in the Blight."

When I look upon Connor again, I find a flicker of surprise on his face. Clearly he wasn't expecting me to say something kind about him after what he just said about me. Maybe he realizes that, despite all of what he's been coached to say, he knows deep down that we share a dark and inevitable secret—the truth about what lives beyond the narrow sea.

He's a part of this, whether he wants to be or not.

"Jennifer Steel," comes the Judge's voice, booming and harsh. "If I have to reprimand you again—"

"You won't." I nod at the Judge with dark, annoyed resolve. "I've said my piece."

"Fine." Judge Enea turns to Connor. "Thank you for your testimony. You are dismissed, Mr. Easton."

Connor shuffles his feet, gives me one last, lingering look of uncertainty, then leaves the podium. I don't even see where he goes, the sight of him robbed from me at this lowly angle.

Judge Enea lifts her chin at me, self-important and full of authority. "The only other witness to your actions is a woman by the name of Dana, whose presence obviously cannot be made here in Court, as she is still stranded in the Blight with the state of her life unknown. And thus, we are now ready to hear your final statement of defense, Jennifer Steel, before the Court adjudicates."

I just want this "formality" of a trial to be over with. Let the paperwork be filled out and filed away. Return me to my boring life so my friends and I can put all of this bureaucratic nonsense behind us.

So I fulfill my part of the deal to President Vale. Again. "I do wish to say something about the Dead."

Dead, dead, dead … My words echo, racing away from me, bigger than my voice will ever be again after today. They inspire an eerie rush of commotion across the entire space of the enormous room. It is much like the sound of wind picking up, and catching with it stray bits of trash as they hiss and gasp and shuffle across the ground.

Judge Enea, her eyes half-lidded and unimpressed with the grandeur of my words—or the effect it had on the sprinkle of people paying witness to this hearing—gives a simple gesture of her hand toward me. "So let us hear it. What have you to say about the Dead?"

I place my hands calmly on the podium. "I wish to state for the record that …" *This isn't easy to say, but I'll say it anyway.* "… the Dead … do not exist. It is true, what Connor attested to. It is true, what they all have said. I recklessly brought my friends—and a few unintended others—with me across the sea. I am the only one to blame, and I acted on my own. Please do not spread the blame of action on my friends John Mason and Marianne Gable. They in fact advised me against what I did. They tried to stop it, but were brought along just as unwillingly as Connor. They do not deserve punishment. They do not deserve judgment."

Pleased with my words, I take a breath, then relax my stance at the podium. I hope that's enough to satisfy whatever dream President Vale was hoping for me to spin for the Judge, the government, and whatever other ears are present for my social and educational demise.

The Judge hardly leaves a moment's room to let my words resonate with anyone at all. "And is that your final statement?"

It's as if she barely heard a word of it.

I take a breath, then give her a nod.

"Very well." She addresses the room now. "Please let it be known in the Court, in the interest of a combined report of all three accused and their testimonies, that John Mason and Marianne Gable, while not in the figurative driving seat of this wildly illegal plan, do share equal parts blame for not having put a stop to it. A responsible peer and proper, loyal student of Skymark University would have been expected to intervene. Consequently, it is the decision of Skymark University in joint agreement with this Court that Mr. Mason's recent enrollment, as well as Ms. Gable's enrollment, as well as Ms. Steel's enrollment have all been permanently terminated. All three of the students in question are hereby permanently banned from Skymark University, as well as any other university where the power of Jurisdictions 10 through 12 preside."

"What??" I blurt out, but whatever was projecting my voice seems to have been silenced, and my words are lost to the boom of Judge Enea's own.

"The Court has arrived at a unanimous decision," the Judge goes on, "which is as follows."

The Judge Supreme then rises from her podium and lifts a smooth, metal scepter, the end of which buzzes with electricity—a Judge Supreme's Gavel of Justice, an item that children fear since their first days of school, an item that can steal away someone's future with just one flick of its ominous, buzzing, sputtering end.

"Jennifer Steel is formally sentenced to twelve years of imprisonment, with no chance of early release, with no rights to visitation or interaction with the outside world in any way or form, and with no chance of appeal."

"JUDGE!" I shriek out, slapping hands to my mouth.

The Gavel of Justice makes a terrible clapping noise as it descends upon the Judge's podium, like thunder rippling across the sky, but tinnier, eerie, and offputting.

The sentence is made final.

And in the noise of the Court erupting into chatter and excited murmurs of scandal, I speak toward the Judge with all the volume I can muster, as my podium is no longer any help. "Please, Judge Enea! Don't do this! I've done *everything* that's been asked of me. I'll do or say anything to stop the riots. I'll give a speech, a far, far more convincing one than my dissertation in the history class. Please, I—*Get your hands off of me!*" The authorities have taken hold of my arms. "Please! Judge!! My mother just lost my father! Don't take me away from her, too! Please! This trial was just supposed to be a formality!!" The Judge has turned away, already gathering her papers for whoever trial follows mine. She isn't hearing a word of this, yet still I scream out: "The president lied to us! President Vale lied to us! I renounce my confessions! I renounce them all!!"

But sooner than I expect, I'm out of the auditorium, and the great metal doors that let me in now shut in my face, taking my words away and leaving me only with the frantic tears on my cheeks.

What just happened?

Winter's Doom

Were John and Mari already sentenced? Were their trials before mine? The Judge said something about all of our testimony being put together.

Did our stories not line up?

Did we do something wrong?

Or did President Vale truly deceive us to get us to confess publicly—yet again—that there was nothing over there but dead trees and nothing?

We round a corner, and I realize it's far from where my previous cell was. "Where are we going?" I ask, out of breath. I don't even remember crying, but the one or two tears—which I'll call "tears of panic" from my shouting at the Court—still sit upon my cheeks, unable to be wiped away since the authorities' grip on my arms robs me of the use of my hands.

They don't answer me anyway.

The farther we walk, the more industrial the halls appear, and soon I feel a draft of wind sweeping up from the floor, cold as a winter front. It isn't until we reach a long stretch of a metal corridor that I see outside through a long thin window, revealing the night sky.

Something about the night air gives me a chill that I cannot shake.

Something isn't right.

"Where are we going?" I asks more sternly.

The authorities gripping my arms say nothing.

Then we pass through a large metal archway that leads to a hovercraft landing site, where no less than six hovercrafts are parked by an enormous door that opens into the night. There are other prisoners, dressed in the same drab grey attire as myself, being directed into the hovercrafts.

Among them, I spot him. "John!!" I cry out. "John!! Over here!"

The moment he hears my voice, he spins and searches for me, fighting off the authorities guiding him onto a hovercraft. His eyes find mine. "Jen!"

"John!!"

But not a second later, he's shoved forcefully into the hovercraft, and my view of him is lost.

"Where are you taking us??" I spit out, pulling against their vice-tight grips. "We're already at the prison! This is the House of Courts and Justice!"

Heedless to my questions, the authorities direct me to a different hovercraft. I stumble up the metal ramp and am dumped into a seat, where I'm promptly strapped down next to another woman, also dressed in grey. Her eyes are full of tears, and she's muttering under her breath over and over, *"I did my best. I did my best. I did my best."*

"What's going on here?" I ask her quietly as the ramp to the hovercraft slaps shut, and the hovercraft hums as it comes to life. "Is there some … other prison facility?"

Winter's Doom

"Seriously?" mutters a young man with sparkling blue eyes from across the aisle, strapped to a chair of his own. A scraggly red beard swallows his mouth as he speaks. "You haven't heard what the government does with us long-term accused? It's called prison overcrowding. And this is their inhumane solution."

"Silence!" shouts one of the nearby guards, and with a threatening lift of his gun, the young bearded man shuts up with a roll of his eyes and looks away, annoyed.

My breath has turned shallow as I cast my gaze to the cold metal floor, terrified.

From my vantage, I barely see a sliver of window, and with it being so late in the night, there is nothing through that glass but blackness. I can't even see stars anymore.

Minutes crawl by. My hands are beginning to cramp from the binds by the time an hour's passed. Then it's two hours and I'm feeling a pang of untimely hunger. My mouth is dry, and my throat is rough from the screaming I did in Court.

I would give anything to be on that other hovercraft with John. Even if we are about to meet some kind of unknowable demise wherever they take us, at least we'd be able to meet it together.

Instead, I get a crazy muttering woman at my side: *"I did my best, I did my best, I did my—"*

"Yes, fine, alright," I snap at her. "You did your best."

"Silence!" comes the guard again.

I glare ahead and grit my teeth.

The next time I see President Rosella Vale and her pretty ruby-red hair and her crisp pantsuit and her scarf, I'm going to murder her.

It isn't a dream. It isn't an idle threat. It isn't some silly passing statement made out of agitation or a thought I'll regret later in a more compassionate state of mind.

It's a promise.

I will kill her.

"Arrived, sir," calls out one of the pilots in the front.

Quite suddenly, the guards start moving around the hovercraft quickly, as if some practiced procedure has been initiated. Then at once, the ramp of the hovercraft opens, and to all our joint horror, we find we're still in the air. Below, we only see darkness.

One of the prisoners, a middle-aged man, is released from the straps of his chair. With little ceremony other than being literally pushed as if by a schoolyard bully, the man is tossed down the ramp, where he then vanishes into the darkness, falling with a scream that's swallowed at once by the hum of the hovercraft engine and the wind.

That's when the real panic sets in.

"What are you doing?!" screams the next one, a lady with long dark hair. "Please, no! No, don't, don't!" But her words are as useful as her pushing at the guards, for five feeble seconds later, she too is thrown out of the hovercraft, disappearing to the depths below.

I blink, stunned.

This is actually happening.

Then comes the young bearded man across from me, whose brave act of defiance earlier is now traded for a look of childlike fear in his bright, sparkly blue eyes, and he begins crying out in a way that can only be compared to a child begging for his mommy. After several useless tugs against the mighty muscles of the guards, he's thrown out of the craft, and his screams go with him.

"I DID MY BEST! I DID MY BEST! I DID—!" shrieks the woman at my side, as if her words can save her the louder she exclaims them, but she is unbound and pulled to the ramp where, in a tumble of screams, she goes too.

And that makes me the next lucky one.

I don't resist when I'm untied from my chair and pulled to my feet. I'm brought to the top of the ramp, and through its yawning mouth, I see swirls of dark mist and unknowable void. Is it the middle of the ocean? Is it a deep canyon? Is it a wintry mountaintop?

"Do I get any last words?" I ask darkly.

Then hands find my back, and I'm thrown from the spot where I stand, tumbling out of the mouth of the craft and into the nothingness.

Chapter Four

Death After Life

The fall lasts exactly two and a half seconds.

I shoulder the fall with a grunt, landing in a spread of grey, ashy sand, which blows across my face from the engine of the hovercraft. When I look up, it's already flying off, leaving me where I've been dumped, and taking the storm of dust with it.

I shield my eyes from the sand, but it doesn't prevent me from coughing my lungs out. I rise to my feet and, once the dust settles, watch the hovercraft disappear over the horizon of water.

Water. Ocean.

I'm on a beach.

Still half-shielding my face, I look around myself, taking in the environment. It's an empty beach of greyish, colorless sand, and in the distance up the coast is a line of thorny, dead trees. Above them hangs a thick blanket of lifeless, stationary fog.

Realization dawns on me. I drop my hand.

Winter's Doom

I'm back in the Blight. The Sunless Reach.

The land of the Dead.

Is that what the blue-eyed bearded guy meant on the hovercraft? Is this what they do with their "long-term prisoners", throw us away in a land that's sure to do us in?

Why not just execute us?

In a total, uncomprehending daze, I start walking the coast, stumbling through the sand. No one is around me. The hovercraft must have never stopped, moving along the coast as they dumped us out one by one, scattering us like bugs. Of course they couldn't be bothered to take us somewhere humane; they didn't want to fly any deeper inland than they had to. Hell, they're probably so afraid of the Dead, they didn't even want to risk the courtesy of parking the hovercraft to escort us off like respectable human beings.

Unfortunately, they spread us so far apart, I can't even see the last person who was thrown off the hovercraft before me. With the waves crashing, I hear little else but the white noise of the beach.

I can't even fathom how far down the coast John must be—or if his hovercraft even let their subjects out on the coast at all. They might've dumped them in the thorny woods, or over a swampy river, or right in the middle of the Whispers for all I know.

Then I hear a man's shout.

I turn. It came from the distant woods.

Was that John??

I hurry across the sand, which is harder than it sounds, each step of the slippery, ashen grey waste pulling at my feet. I kick up sand as I scramble hurriedly toward the old grey trees. "John??" I call out. "John??"

Before I know it, I'm in the thick of the woods in pursuit of the shout—and am reminded all too much of our first visit here when our stolen hovercraft crashed in the middle of these dark, daunting, lifeless trees. The welcome we got from the Dead was less than kind.

It's only been a week. Would they remember us if we encountered them again? Would they welcome us back?

Or would they be too hungry for blood to tell the difference between us?

"John!" I call out into the darkness.

The lifeless trees stare back at me, silent and cold.

I swear to myself I won't be lost, not like I was the last time I was here. In fact, as soon as I start recognizing the lay of the land—assuming I'm anywhere *near* the spot I was when I first arrived here—I should be able to find my way to After's Hold, the city I spent a night or so in with my friends. We were protected there by the "civilized" Dead who had no taste for our blood, ruled over by the Mayor Damnation (who was taller than any woman I'd ever met) and her friend Truce, a curious one who looked powdered and made-up more than my grandma used to be during the holiday season—*and that's saying quite a lot.* Diviner Dana should also still be there, assuming she's survived this long.

I just have to find my friends.

Before something else does.

But ten minutes later, there is still no sight of him—or anyone, for that matter. "John?" I try one last, feeble time, my voice wimpy and lost to the dark.

No one and nothing responds.

I stop under one of the trees, back myself against it, and listen. Nothing reaches my ears, not even the slightest pull of wind nor crunch of a twig beneath a foot.

Instinctively, my hand plunges into my pocket.

The stone is still there.

I pull it out and fiddle with it nervously as my eyes continue scoping all around me, searching for the faintest sign of movement. It isn't an easy feat at night in the land of the Dead. The only light I have is a wash of dull moonlight that somehow diffuses its way through the permanent blanket of fog overhead, spilling faintly along the shapes of things, leaving the world before my eyes indistinct, eerily silhouetted, and colorless.

I know what I *have* lost sight of: the beach. I went so deep into the woods in pursuit of the shouting, I've lost all sense of direction.

This place has a way of doing that.

Making one lose oneself.

Didn't I just promise myself I wouldn't get lost? Of course I'd break my first and only promise to myself.

Then: "Are you alive?"

I jerk away from the tree at the sound of the words, grab a branch straight off the ground, and face the speaker of the words with my makeshift weapon brandished before me threateningly.

He takes a step into the clearing. Soft moonlight falls upon his face.

I lower my branch. "The poet from campus," I realize with a start.

Indeed, the one who named himself Grim stands there in the trees, pale and black of hair, his wide eyes curious and careful. His slender build makes him seem as thin and lifeless as the trees around us, which would make me suspect that he's actually a Dead, if it weren't for the flush of his cheeks at the sight of me. This one's alive, I'm sure.

"Jennifer," he murmurs for a greeting, relieved. "It *is* you. Oh, wow."

I put a few things together rather quickly in my mind. "You were arrested. They put you through a trial, like me. You were sentenced and dropped off here by hovercraft."

"Yes, alas," he confirms sullenly. "You, too?"

I nod.

Winter's Doom

He comes further into the small clearing I stand in, then peers up, as if to check the sky for something. It causes the moonlight to fall differently on his face, accenting his angular features. Grim is an unusual kind of handsome, as equally appealing as he is peculiar and odd.

"We should keep moving," he decides, then brings his soft gaze back down to mine. "We're bound to run into the others who were dropped in this area."

It occurs to me suddenly that Grim wasn't on my hovercraft. *Does that mean …?* "Did you see my friends, by chance? The ones I was with by the fountain? John? Or Mari, the one who stabbed herself in the head with a knife during my presentation? Were they on your hovercraft?"

Grim wrinkles his lips, then sadly shakes his head no.

I take a steeling breath. I need to be strong out here, just like I was the first time. "We're bound to run into the others," I agree. "Your friends and mine."

"I have no friends." Grim offers me a tentative smile. "Well, unless I might call you one. Though, while I might know *of* you, and you of me, we actually know little of each other. Isn't that funny?"

"No," I answer dryly. At the sight of his stunned face, I amend my statement with: "But perhaps when our lives aren't in danger, I might find things funny again."

He purses his lips, then averts his gaze. "Right."

"Let's get moving."

"Moving, yes, smart," he agrees, then smiles again.

The pair of us pass through the dark trees blindly. The unfortunate side effect of having someone else with me is how much *louder* we are crossing through these woods. It seems like Grim's feet find every possible twig and branch to crunch and snap as we walk. I know he isn't doing it on purpose, but could he just exercise a little more caution?

"Is it strange that I'm actually *excited* we're here?"

Since I'm walking ahead of him leading the way, I give an unseen roll of my eyes. "Considering we could die at any second or get eaten by a Dead, yes, I find it strange."

"Sorry." He gives a light, breathy chuckle. "I've been fascinated with the strange and the bizarre since I was a child. Maybe it's why I'm a poet. Back in school, I had a lot of trouble making friends. My mother and father were artists, you see, and I—"

Lovely. Now I get to suffer hearing his whole sad backstory. "Sorry, Grim, but I just want to find my friends and get somewhere safe," I tell him, cutting him off.

"Yes, of course," Grim agrees. "You're right."

"And if we keep talking and making noise," I go on, "it might draw them to us. Silence is key in these lands."

"Of course." He makes a gesture as if to lock his lips and toss the key. Then his eyes light up and whatever imaginary lip-lock he made is broken at once. "Wait. You mean *them*-them? Like … the *Dead* them?"

Winter's Doom

I sigh and ignore his question, pushing on.

Grim wisely doesn't pursue the matter.

We walk another ten or so minutes in silence, which is remarkable considering how *chatty* he was a moment ago. I keep my eyes wide and unblinking in the dark, which has helped them adjust, drinking in whatever tiny tendrils of light lurk in the forest.

"What breath the wind of this world draws through its lifeless branches ..." murmurs Grim whimsically, *"yet for only the benefit of those whose lungs draw none."*

I don't respond to his poetry. I'm tired, I'm hungry, and I'm slowly losing hope with every minute that drags by in these dark, desolate woods.

"Hmm ... *'benefit'*? No, maybe it's *'grace'* I'm looking for. *'Yet for only the* grace *of those whose lungs draw none.'* Yes, rolls a bit better off the tongue. Or is it *'delight'* I'm hearing instead? *'Yet for only the* delight *of—"*

Quite suddenly, I've had enough of Grim. "Do you realize you're part of the reason we're all here?"

He appears stunned. "How do you mean?"

"Your passionate speeches. Your inciting people to take action with the government or the school. Your ..." I gesture at him agitatedly. "... *annoying zeal!*"

Grim lifts his eyebrows. "But don't you want the world to know the truth? Don't you resent the school making you bury it with lies and falsehood?"

"Of course I resent the school and the government," I blurt out, "but I also value my life and my friends' lives, and I know that I'm just one powerless person, and that government is *legion* and *all-powerful*. How is measly me supposed to stand up to all of that? And now look where I am." I kick a nearby tree in frustration. "Back among the Dead." Then I add with a snort: "And *they* aren't even nearby to welcome us. Maybe even the *Dead* are dead."

Grim frets anxiously. "But … But you stood up to the government the day you took a hovercraft right out from under their noses and flew it over here. That's the truth of what happened, right?" Grim comes up close to me as his voice lowers—*as if anyone else is actually listening to this*. "It had nothing to do with that Dana person, did it? It was all you, wasn't it?"

This Grim character is particularly intuitive.

And annoying. "It doesn't matter anymore."

"Of course it matters. Our government abolished the death penalty centuries ago, so now they've resorted to doing the next worst thing they can imagine: banishing us to a world they're certain we can't survive." He gives me an important look. "But *you* did."

I cross my arms. "I survived out of sheer *luck*, and I did so with my friends at my side."

"And you'll do more than survive this time. Don't you realize, Jennifer? *This* is your home." He spreads his hands and gazes up at the sky. *"Oh, but for the fog that hangs o'er our weary heads like a babe's blanket, swaddled in death's grey love, a wreath of hidden truth, a crown of ascent.* Yes, yes, this place will certainly be our making, not our unmaking. Oh, Jennifer, the government were fools not to keep us there under their control."

My anger toward him has quickly turned to pity. This poet is a lost cause of dreams, with a head full of delusion about what the Dead really are. And once he learns, his whole world will change, and he'll realize why I'm not in the least happy to be back in these woods.

But it's difficult to stay mad at someone so passionate and driven by his dreams. I wish I still had mine.

He won't last long here without me.

"They were fools to send us here," I agree.

Grim looks at me, then a smile finds his oddly pallid face. "Yes. Fools, indeed."

At once, the unmistakable sound of a deep-throated growl comes from the darkness.

Grim and I turn, alarmed.

The growl persists, though no body yet accompanies the menacing sound.

"Is it one of them?" Grim asks me—and even now, his question is asked half in fear, half in delighted fascination.

Something in the dark breaks into a sprint.

"No time to find out!" I exclaim at Grim. "Run!"

At once, the pair of us dart through the darkness. The grass is crunchy and oddly slippery, making me feel as if the Dead world is greedily grabbing hold of my feet.

In the near total darkness, I can barely see where my next step is. The woods are unfairly thick in these parts, filled with unseen roots daring to trip us and obstacles that appear before our faces in mere seconds. It makes the act of racing away from an unknown pursuer all the more perilous.

A pursuer that keeps growling and snapping its jaws.

A wolf? A wild dog? Some deadly beast prowling the Dead woods in desperate pursuit of flesh just as hungrily as the Dead themselves?

Suddenly the trees break away, and a vast field opens before us, painted in pale moonlight. Ahead, I spot what might be a rice silo—a giant cylindrical building made of metal with a door at its base.

The growling and snapping of jowls grows closer and closer to our heels.

At once, I'm upon the door, nearly slamming into it as I fumble with the handle to get the creaky metal thing open. "It's stuck!" I shriek, yanking on the wide lever of a handle with psychotic desperation, unable to turn it.

Then Grim appears, out of breath, and shoves himself into the muscular effort of turning the lever.

And it gives, the door opening.

Winter's Doom

The pair of us slip inside and pull shut the door at our backs. Not a second later, a resonant *bang* indicates the beast crashing into the door, where it then barks and growls and snaps its jaws, desperate for a bite of one of us.

Grim and I back away from the door, catching our breaths. "What was that thing??" breathes Grim, wide-eyed. I shake my head, unable to answer. I didn't even get a proper look at it.

Grim turns around. "Oh, look."

I follow his gaze, peering upward. There is a crude metal staircase that spirals up the throat of the rice silo, ending at a landing up top where moonlight seems to spill in, indicating an opening of some kind.

"Maybe it'll give us a good vantage point," Grim points out. "I imagine we can see a lot from up there. Maybe we could even spot where to go next."

"Good. Alright." I make my way for the stairs, still catching my breath. After one last lingering look at the door, listening to the growls and whimpers of the wild animal, Grim follows behind me.

It's a minute or two before we reach the top.

It's a lot of stairs.

But when we do, we find ourselves on a large, wide landing that looks like the penthouse to some lofty, high-dollar hotel, except they've stripped away all the nice furniture, the wall décor, and the carpet. Everything here

71

is a rusty metal color, and the odor of iron and rust is so strong, it almost smells of dried blood. At the far end of the room, the entire wall is torn out, like a wide floor-to-ceiling glassless window—a balcony of sorts.

Reaching the precipice, I stare out at the landscape beyond. Dilapidated warehouses stand in the distance, surrounded by areas of cages and metal fences, reminding me of the animal hospitals and pet adoption centers back home, containing big cages and pens where animals live. I spot what looks like a factory or two in the distance, but the exhaust pipes that reach into the sky let out no smoke, and all around them are spreads of mud and dust and half-fallen buildings.

"I don't recognize this place," I say sullenly.

Grim, who stands many paces behind me, only crosses his arms and mutters, "Very … *industrial.* Smoggy. Old."

"Old," I agree. "Like in our history books. Reminds me of the Industrial Era of many millennia ago." I glance over my shoulder. "What're you doing all the way back there?"

"I, um …" He shuffles his feet uncomfortably. "I don't do well with, um … with heights." He takes yet another step back, putting more distance between himself and the wide, gaping, banister-free balcony at which I stand.

I smirk, then glance down, curious if I might find the beast circling the tower from down there. I see nothing.

Winter's Doom

"This is just … just a more elaborate death sentence," Grim decides, muttering nervously as he keeps sneaking glances at the opening, then looking away. "Sending us here. Honoring their no-death-sentence law and keeping their hands clean. I really do hate our government."

I peer back at him. "You're really so afraid of heights?"

"The potential of heights. How far one can … fall. Just the thought of … of falling. Even if I were to get close enough to drop something … to … to *lose* something …" Grim shudders and takes yet another step away from the ledge, then eyes me. "Can you not stand so close?"

I lift an eyebrow. "Really? I'm making you nervous?"

"Overwhelmingly. Please, just take a few steps back. The wind here is erratic, and it could take just one gust of it to—"

"Need I remind you that this was *your* idea," I point out, "to come up here and get a better vantage?"

"Yes, but …" He fidgets, bites his finger, then points at the balcony. "But I didn't expect it to not at least have a *railing of some kind* to protect us."

I sit down where I am, a few feet from the edge, cross-legged with my hands in my lap. "Is this better?"

Grim's thin eyebrows pull together. "Not much. Tell me about John."

"What?"

"John. Tell me about him to distract me. Who is he?"

I blink. What an odd subject to bring up with a person I barely know. "John is … my boyfriend. And roommate. Unofficially."

"Unofficially your roommate? Or … unofficially your boyfriend?"

I give it an honest thought. With the way John and I stand, and the slight ambiguity of our relationship, I'm not quite sure. It took the dire circumstances of being near the Whispers for John and I to finally admit our feelings for one another, but since then, we've both been emotional ghosts. So much has happened. So much is still happening. Will we ever just find a peace that's our own, that no one and nothing else will try to tear apart?

"I don't know the answer to that question," I reply. "Maybe. Maybe not. I just don't know."

"Hmm." He sits down, too, then hugs his knees to his chest and leans back against the wall. "Maybe it isn't moving to the next step for a reason. It's human, to be unsure of things, to question everything. Has anyone ever told you how beautiful your hair is?"

I flinch at the sudden compliment, then glance over at him. I find his soft eyes observing me, curious, ponderous.

"It's white," I return dryly to him. "No one has hair this white. Not even great grandparents."

"I think it's beautiful."

"And don't presume to understand John and I."

Winter's Doom

Grim parts his lips, then frowns. "I-I'm sorry, I—"

"We have each other's hearts. We are in this together, he and I. It's the world that keeps pulling us apart. The university, for not having accepted his enrollment in the first place. The government, for criminalizing my interest in the Dead. And now we've both been returned here to the land of the Dead, lost and hopeless."

"You're not lost. And you're not hopeless."

"Oh, what do you know?" I snap suddenly. "A poet who dreams things. A poet who *wants* things. A poet who is in love with the Dead, but you've not yet met one. Oh, but when you do ... ha!" I let out an untimely, dark laugh and shake my head. "You'll wish you never uttered a word in my direction, that much I promise you."

"But you're home," he insists yet again. "This isn't where you're lost, Jennifer Steel."

I flick him a challenging look of my eyes.

Grim smiles. "This is where you're found."

My look falters.

I realize I'm still holding the rock. I must've clung to it the entire time we ran away from that mysterious beast I never got a proper look at. Unable to look at Grim, I cast my gaze to the stone and turn it over a few times in my palm, staring at it with determination.

"Maybe the wild animal's gone," Grim suggests softly. "We could go back down and see."

"Or stay up here forever," I mutter tiredly, turning the stone over and over in my hand. "We could stay up here and stare out at the world and wait for any of the others to find us."

"What're you playing with?"

I sigh sourly. "A useless, nothing rock, that's what."

Just after I say the words, the rock seems to turn cold in my hands. I wince, yet stubbornly refuse to let it go. It's like I'm holding an ice cube suddenly.

"What's that noise?" asks Grim with alarm, rising off the ground and taking a few steps toward the ledge, as close as he dares to come.

I lift my eyes from the stone, then turn around and gaze over the precipice at the ground below.

Across the entire span of cracked dirt and dust that spreads out from the base of our tower, arms and hands have burst out of the earth. Those arms slowly become bodies as they claw their way free—tens of them, then dozens more, and hundreds—and before our horrified eyes, countless Undead are standing below us, encircling the tower, grunting and moaning and crying out.

And each and every one of their decrepit, rotted, Dead faces—the ones who *have* faces—gaze upwards at the tower, all of them staring directly at me.

Chapter Five

An Ocean Of Faces

"We're so, so dead," hisses Grim, wide-eyed, staring down at the ocean of faces.

"No," I say, just as stunned as he is. *"They* are."

"What do we do?"

"Nothing. They can't get up here. The door—"

"It wasn't locked, Jennifer." Grim's eyes are on mine. "If any of them have basic motor functions and brains, they can literally walk right in and climb the stairs. We're trapped, Jennifer. We're—" His eyes fall on the stone in my grasp again. "Seriously, what is that rock?"

I wrinkle my face, then hug the rock to my chest. "It's just a keepsake I brought from home."

"Are you sure? It seems like ..." Grim glances out at the field of Dead, then back at me, wide-eyed. "Did *you* do this? Are you raising the Dead?"

I open my mouth, then find I've been utterly struck speechless. I pull the stone back out of my pocket and gaze on it again, baffled beyond words.

"Where did you say you got that again?"

"I …" I'm still staring at it, confounded. "I got it at the gardens. The day John and I met. We stole it, actually."

"Stole it?"

"Yeah. I dropped it on our way out of the gardens, and the flowers it dropped on … they … they died."

"Died …" Grim bites his lip, appearing worried.

That's when I hear the chanting, pulling both our gazes out to the unsightly crowd below. They all chant a word … a name … and they chant it in a blood-chilling, perfect unison, like all of those Dead down there share one mind, one consciousness, one great soul split into a thousand Undead slivers:

Winter … Winter … Winter … Winter …

I swear the crowd has doubled in size since we first saw them break from the ground. *Winter … Winter … Winter …* And each and every one of them peers up at the tower, some of them on their knees, some of them raising their hands up as if wishing to touch me, to revere me, to worship me. *Winter … Winter …*

"It's like you're their leader, their *goddess*," murmurs Grim, wide-eyed. "I think you're home now, Jennifer."

"This isn't my home."

"But they've clearly been waiting for you. Look!"

Suddenly I can't stand the chanting. Still crouched on the rusty floor, I grip the edge of the precipice, lean over it, and shout down at them, "I'm not Winter!! You are all mistaken! Stop chanting that damn name! It's not me!"

At my words, all the Dead draw silent.

The chanting has been traded now for a soundless, eerie, piercing nothingness.

I swallow.

Maybe I should have preferred the chanting.

Then a sole figure moves through the crowd—a Dead I didn't until now notice at all. When she walks, the others part, making way for her, and when she stops, she lifts her smooth, bald head and peers up at me.

It's her. The female Dead with the one eye.

Corpsey's sister.

"Who's that?" whispers Grim. *"Do you know her?"*

I frown. "You can say that."

The sister calmly approaches the tower—the Dead still parting to make way for her—then she's out of sight.

A noise from below suggests the opening of a door.

"She's coming up," hisses Grim.

Thank you, Captain Obvious.

I rise from the floor and turn just as the bald woman comes into view at the top of the stairs. She is joined by a few Dead flanking her as she calmly crosses the room.

When she comes to a stop several paces away, that's when I notice who the companion at her side is.

Corpsey himself.

Despite being Dead, he's got an alluringly innocent, childlike look in his eyes, like he's always afraid to offend someone. Yet the peculiar way his mouth curls suggests how easily capable he would be to tear out someone's throat with his teeth, if they crossed him the wrong way.

He saved my life once or twice last time I was here.

I saved his Unlife in return.

Our relationship is complicated.

"Winter," says the sister, softly and with strange, wet adoration in her eyes. "I *knew* you'd come back."

I swallow and take an instinctive step backwards—which only reminds me that there is a ledge on my heel. One more step will send me falling.

Quite suddenly, I share Grim's fear of heights.

"I've not come back willingly," I respond. "I've been banished here. By my own kind. And it's because of what I've publicly said to them about … about my time here."

She tilts her head and squints her one eye, confused. "How do you mean?"

"They don't want people to know you exist."

"Ah." She smirks. "Sounds like the Old Trentonite philosophy, except … opposite. *Deny the Dead to protect the Living* … and you Trentonites used to deny the Living to protect the Dead." Her mouth curls with amusement, and a single dry chuckle escapes it. "What blissful humor."

Just get to the point. "What're you going to do to me?"

Winter's Doom

The cold nature of my question catches her off-guard. She looks confused. *"Do to you …?"* She glances at her brother, who has been staring at me with a blank, stony expression since he arrived. *"She still thinks we wish to harm her? Why so?"*

Corpsey remains as still as a mannequin, only his lips moving when he replies, *"Because when we last saw her, I betrayed her to you, stole her not-steel item with the pictures in it, and you made to kill her until she uttered Winter's words."*

His sister nods slowly. *"Ah, yes. The words."* Her one eye flicks back to me. *"'You did this to yourself. The only one left to blame is you.' Of course. Winter, you're waking."*

"I'm not Winter, and I'm plenty awake."

"Fine. You can call yourself whatever you want," she says with a shrug. *"It is all the same to us Dead."*

And then she drops to one knee.

The others behind her follow suit. The thuds of bony knees hitting the floor echo down the tall rice silo. Even Corpsey drops to one knee, but he then lifts his gaze to meet mine, curious of my reaction, perhaps.

It isn't an interesting reaction. I just stand there and stare down at them, dumbfounded.

Then Grim and I share a look, unsure what to do.

And quite suddenly, I no longer wish to be backed precariously to the ledge of a very tall tower anymore.

I want to be reunited with my friends.

And the only way to do that is to get as far from here as I possibly can. "I need a word with you in private."

The sister looks up at me, then spreads her hands. "You're standing before my most trusted. Whatever it is you wish to say to me, you can say right here."

"I prefer not to."

"You're wondering why we're kneeling," the sister decides, then smiles. "Winter, we're ready."

I'm fast losing patience. "Ready for what?"

"The great Revolution, of course!"

Grim stares at me in wonder. "R-Revolution …?"

I return his look with a shrug. *How should I know what that means?*

The sister, quite suddenly less cordial, flicks her eye at Grim, annoyed. "And who's this *other Human* with you?"

"He's a friend," I answer her. "You can trust him."

She purses her lips, seeming unconvinced. "Alright," she grunts anyway, then turns her eye back onto me. "Yes, the great Revolution, as I said. We have been ready for the Revolution for quite some time. We are armed. We are trained. And all the rest of us are beginning to wake, too, all ten thousand of us. We—"

"TEN THOUSAND??"

My words explode out of the tower and echo across the field of countless Dead, much like they did through the podium microphone during my trial—*Ten thousand, ten thousand, ten thousand …*

I swallow down the rest of my shock and force myself to speak more civilly. "Sorry. I'm … I was a bit …" I run a hand through my hair, gathering my composure. "I was a bit *startled* by the sheer number of … gathering Dead you just mentioned. Ten thousand, you said? Are you sure? Never mind, don't answer that. *Phew, I doubt we even have five thousand people at the university alone.*"

The sister squints at me. "Uni … versity …?"

An unfamiliar word on this side of the ocean, perhaps. "A school. A place where we learn things. Where I'm from. Never mind. I still need to speak to you in private."

"About what?" she asks. "Us? You want to know all about us and how I know you and why your name carries such power on the lips and eyes of every Dead? Oh, there's so much to say, Winter, I might as well just show you." She rises off the ground, then gives a flick of her wrist at the others behind her. "Leave, please. Give her some space. Erick," she then says, turning to her brother. "Let's take her to the *tomb*."

Erick … So that's his real name.

He lifts his eyes to meet mine, seeming curious about something. Then he gives a grunt, nods, and turns away.

"Can we trust them?" whispers Grim, tugging on the sleeve of my grey prison shirt. *"Should we follow them?"*

"I don't know, and I don't know," I answer back, then follow the Dead as they descend down the stairs. Grim is right on my heels, though it's difficult to discern whether he's excited or terrified at everything that's unfolding.

Probably excited.

Now I know how all my friends felt when I excitedly announced my main focus of study was to be the Dead.

That was long before I actually knew what they were like.

Once outside the rice silo and safely back on the ground, we enter a whole new nightmare of unsurpassed horror: walking directly through a thick, massive crowd of Dead—each of them with their eyes glued upon us with equal parts wonder and lip-licking hunger.

I am, in this tiny moment, very grateful for Erick and his sister.

Ugh. Calling him Erick feels weird. I'll stick with Corpsey.

"In here," directs the sister as we reach a pair of cellar doors, which reveal stone steps that run deep.

What have we to lose? I keep following, Grim right at my back, nearly breathing down my neck for as close as he keeps to me.

"This is the tomb," the sister introduces us, gesturing at the walls and the labyrinthine corridors, which are lit by tiny, insufficient torches that still cause me to squint to see anything properly. "Down here, written across the walls, is our story. This whole place has a history—a long

Winter's Doom

and terrible one—which happens to be directly related to you and your mother."

That catches me by surprise. "My mother? What does she have to do with this?"

"Oh, well ... Perhaps it's more accurate if I were to say *Winter's* mother. I don't know if your *current* mother is the same, or ..." She sighs and gives a careless gesture of her bony hand. "I don't know how it all works, your whole coming back for a Third Life. Or Fourth Life. Or whatever this is. You've read about it all in your books, haven't you? 'The Beautiful Dead', my brother told me you called us." She chuckles that same offputting, dry chuckle of hers. "I wonder if you've ever read stories about the Necropolis and the Deathless who inhabited it."

Neither word is familiar. "No," I answer, still peering around at everything my eyes can find.

The claustrophobically narrow passageway opens to a small, oblong stone chamber, and it's here that a great brazier burns in the center of the room, casting firelight across all the walls. Upon the stone bricks, I see etchings in white paint and chalk of people, of animals, of knobby trees and a sun beaming over them. I see people battling each other in a large, overgrown forest. I see drawings of big spiders, and one in particular that looks like a woman with spider legs. I see a tall mountain with a tree on top of it, and a squiggly snowfall at its foot.

85

All of the drawings are white and colorless—save one at the opposite end of the chamber, which is a spattering of paint in a deep, rich, vibrant green.

The sight stops me in my tracks.

The green paint is in the shape of an eye.

"Well, welcome to the Necropolis," says the sister, coming to a stop by the brazier, "and the tomb in which its secrets rest. So you said you wished to speak to me in private?" Her brother stops next to her and stares into the flames of the brazier himself, looking glum and pensive.

"You're alright, Jennifer," whispers Grim into my ear. *"These two look like they worship you. I ... I think we can trust them. You're like their queen or something."*

"We can hear you clearly," says the sister from across the room. "Undead hearing is *pristine*. And you're right. Winter *can* trust us. But she didn't need *you* to tell her."

Grim fidgets, blushing.

But it doesn't matter. Quite suddenly, I'm hanging on that one word he just uttered.

Queen.

Maybe Corpsey's sister here is the "queen of them all" that Professor Praun referred to in his message he wanted relayed through me. Maybe she is the one who will know what the cryptic words mean.

And so, standing before the green paint on the wall, I start to recite the words: "The Green Eye opens ..."

Then, just as quickly, I draw silent.

Something inside stops me—something protective, wary, and suspicious of everything.

What if it isn't in my best interest to relay the message to her? *What if Professor Praun had some devious reason for passing on the words—some reason I don't yet know? Can I even trust him, my own professor?*

The sister blinks her one eye, then glances over at her brother, confused. *"The Green Eye opens ...?"* she murmurs quietly to him. *"What does that mean ...?"*

Corpsey stares blankly at me. To his sister's question, he merely shrugs.

Perhaps I'll do this one piece at a time. There's no sense in telling her the rest of the words if she can't make sense of the first. "Yes," I insist more confidently, then turn to face the pair of them. "The Green Eye opens."

The sister meets my gaze and turns her question onto me now. "But what does that mean? Is that ... a riddle? Why do you speak of the Green Eye?"

With one lazy finger, I point up at the wall. "Is this the Green Eye? And ..." *I feel so weird.* "... is it ... *opened* yet?"

She looks back and forth between the wall and my finger, looking more confounded by the second. "I ... It isn't ... It's ..." She clears her throat and composes herself. "The Green Eyes are gone. Each and every one of them. No one has seen a Green Eye in these lands for centuries."

Her answer causes me to freeze.

She knows what the Green Eye is, and there was apparently more than one of them. Green Eyes, plural.

She just said so much with so little.

I glance back at the wall in renewed wonder. Above the eye, a sun shines down through a chalky squiggle of clouds. I bite the inside of my cheek, uncertain. *The Green Eye opens when the Yellow closes. The White has arrived …*

Maybe it's useless, the message. Maybe I'm too late. Apparently there aren't any Green Eyes left to speak of.

Then there comes a soft voice from the dark corridor behind me. "J-Jennifer …? Is that you?"

I know that voice.

I turn around at once, and my eyes fall on her as she slowly emerges into the flickering light of the chamber. "Mari," I breathe with deep relief, then rush up to her and throw my arms around her. "I thought I lost you!"

"I'm here," she says over my shoulder as I crush her soft, round body with my desperate embrace. "Ooh, this is an especially tight hug. Ooh, it tickles!"

"I'm just glad you're okay. I'm …" Then the thought belatedly clicks in place. I pull away and get a look at her. "What are you doing here? With them?"

"I …" Mari bites her lip apprehensively, then glances over at Corpsey and his sister, as if seeking the answer from one of them.

Winter's Doom

And indeed, it comes from the sister: "She found us when the Living ... *deposited* her nearby. They flung her from one of your big metal birds, poor thing. I recognized her from before and took her in."

"Took her in?" I peer back and forth between them, unsettled. "No, she's not staying. She's coming with me."

"But Jennifer ..." protests Mari.

I look at Mari severely, then lower my voice. "*You don't want to stay here with them, Mari. You're my friend, and you'll remember that fact as soon as you have your Waking Dream thing, remember? We need to stick together right now.*"

"We *are* together right now," Mari insists.

"*But not here.*"

"Jennifer, I ..." She starts wringing her hands—*click, click, click.* "I ... I like it here. I'm with my own kind now. They're the ones who ... who made me."

"Um, no," I cut in. "Mr. and Mrs. *Gable* made you. Your mother and father. Through a private little act that happens behind a closed bedroom door. *You were not made here, Marianne.*"

"My new name is Marigold."

I stare at her, incredulous. "Mari—"

"—gold," she finishes again, then smiles. "It's kind of the same, but it feels better. Doesn't it? I like gold things."

"You *hate* gold things," I spit back, annoyed. "You like glowing makeup. You like *silver* and *stainless steel*, Mari."

"Oh, no, you won't find one *bit* of steel around here," interjects the sister. "I assure you that we—"

"I know all about your vulnerability to steel," I snap at the sister, causing her to step back, affronted, "and I am *not* afraid to use it to my advantage if I have to."

A cold and steely silence (pun intended) befalls the tomb after my words are said. And down every corridor, I hear the echoes die tiny deaths, as if racing away to warn every Dead in this place of my deep, daring threat.

Corpsey, the only one unmoved by my big dramatic words, places a calming hand on his sister's shoulder. "Perhaps you should take Marigold to discuss strategies with the others. I will stay with Winter and her friend."

"Fine." The sister, visibly shaken, her one eye looking as if it might fall right out of her face in silent outrage, calmly comes to Mari's side to take her hand. "I'll return, Winter. We can ... chat more about this *Green Eye*. I was so ..." She looks pained for a second, as if her next words hurt to say. "I was ... so looking forward to this day that we would at long last meet again as equals. For years and years and years, I longed for it. I see now the delusions of a child's foolish wishes. Nothing is ever as one dreams it to be. I ... I should have ... lowered my expectations." With that, she calmly departs with Mari.

And I watch Mari go away. My friend. My roommate. *My total stranger.*

Winter's Doom

"I'm sorry."

I glance at Corpsey, the one who just quietly uttered the apology. With his head slightly bowed, staring at me in his curious, half-ghoulish, half-innocent way, he seems genuinely remorseful for how I must be feeling.

And that's giving him a lot of credit, considering what he's done, and how he so easily betrayed me the last time I was here. "Mari is … *was* my friend," I start.

"She still is."

"But she's nothing like her past self. She doesn't know me. She doesn't know the years we shared together. She doesn't know the—*ugh*—the awful ex-boyfriends we have endured and commiserated over, the tears we've had, the laughter, all of the long, long summers we spent out at my countryside home. It's all gone. What's left now?"

"She's safe, at least. You can take comfort in that." He gazes into the fire. "She knows about the Revolution, too. She was told everything. She … wants to be a part of it. When you're ready, of course."

"I won't be ready. I don't even know what the *hell* you guys are talking about. Revolution?"

"Yes. It's what we have waited hundreds of years for." Corpsey turns his gaze onto me, his dull eyes flickering with the light from the dancing flames. "When we take the world back for our own."

"Really? 'Take the world back' …?"

"Yes." He steps away from the fire and approaches me. I'm comfortable enough around him, even now, even after everything, that the thought to step away from him doesn't even cross my mind. "You remember that day just as well as I do. I know you do."

"What day?"

"The day the Whispers spoke to us."

He stops in front of me, taller than me by a foot, and his voice is so low, it's nearly a hiss.

And yes, I heard everything those creepy Whispers said. I know my existence is supposed to be some kind of "symptom" that the end of the world is coming. I know there have been many Winters before me.

I just simply refuse to believe any of that crap.

"Maybe it's a choice," I counter just as softly, staring up at his face, unafraid. "The end of the world. What if I hold the choice in my hands? What if I can stop it?"

"But why would you want to? Winter, your very own people have thrown you away. Cast you off like a piece of trash. *We* are your people now. We've always been your people. We have waited a thousand years for you."

I sigh and tiredly grip my head, frustrated.

Meanwhile, Grim has been so silent, I nearly forgot he was here with us. He still stands near the painting of the big green eye across the room. I can't imagine what sense he's making out of all of this, if anything at all. I wouldn't be surprised if this is the time at which he finally decides he's had enough of the Dead.

When I let go of my head and look up, Corpsey still stands before me, but his eyes have dropped to my lips, a curious, pained look in them.

Then my thoughts take a different direction. "Are you going to be mad if I insist on calling you Corpsey? The name Erick just … sits funny on my tongue."

Surprisingly, he cracks a smile. "I guess it isn't much different than us being made to call you Jennifer."

I smile, too. "No, it isn't."

"Even if your real name is Winter."

My smile fades.

"You may never remember my sister," he goes on, his tone turning grave, "but you two were close. You were like sisters yourselves. And one day, I think it will all come back to you. Maybe you'll even remember how furious you got at her for taking out her own eye."

I stare at him, aghast. "She took out her own—?"

"Yes. I've heard the story several times."

"But why would she do that?"

"Because she had one of these," he answers simply, producing something from his back pocket.

A green, glowing stone.

My eyes grow wide. *Is that …?*

"I thought your sister said—?"

"This is my secret." He averts his gaze and bites his lip, troubled. "For now. I ... I'm not sure why I've kept this from her. I think I'm afraid of what it can do, of what it's capable of. But ... I can't manage to do much with it at all, except ..." He peers up at me, his soft, curious eyes meeting mine, and he says nothing more.

I frown. "Except what?"

"I know you have a stone, too."

I fight an instinct to put my hand in my pocket, as if to protect the very thing he just spoke of. I neither confirm nor deny his claim, staring at him questioningly. Really, how could he possibly know, anyway?

He smirks, appearing smart. "I know you have one because ... I can see you through it."

"You can *what*?"

He lifts the green stone to his eye, then squints into it, as if peering through a telescope. "It's dark, wherever your rock is," he tells me. "Maybe it's ... hidden? I'd say it's in your pocket, if I had to make a guess."

I squirm for all of five seconds before finally relenting. I pull the dull, dark rock out. "This thing?"

His eyes fall onto it. He looks strangely disappointed. "Hmm. It isn't glowing."

"It isn't anything," I throw back. "This rock doesn't do anything. And I can't see anything through it, though ..."

"Though ...?"

Winter's Doom

I shift uncomfortably, then glance over at Grim, who is paying attention to every word of this, fascinated. He has taken to leaning against the wall, his arms folded, and he gives me an encouraging nod from across the room.

"Though, I've ... *I feel funny saying this* ... I've felt like the stone has been watching me." I look at Corpsey. "Was that you I was sensing, then? Watching me through this rock somehow?"

"Perhaps." His fingers close around his green rock, stealing all of its light away. "And now you've come here speaking of a Green Eye opening. I wonder if this is that Green Eye you spoke of. Why *did* you say that earlier?"

As much as I trust Corpsey, I've learned my lesson not to say anything to him I don't want getting back to his sister. He's betrayed me once to her; I'll be considerate enough not to put him in a situation to do that again.

"I read it in a book," I lie straight through my Living teeth, then quickly pocket my own stone. "I'm sorry to do this to you, but whether you like it or not, I'm going to have to get out of here and find John."

He nods slowly. "I figured you would. You know my sister will come after you, right?"

"You think that'll stop me?"

"No. Nothing can stop Winter." He crouches in place, then lazily runs a hand along the top of the fire, the hot tongues of flames lapping at his palm. He gently retracts his hand and peers over his shoulder at me. "Maybe I'm a little less invested in this than my sister. After all, I never knew Winter. I only heard the stories for years and years, and I don't mind much staying here and not engaging in any Revolution that might bring about countless deaths." His eyes turn dark. "But this, I do know: It was *my* death that inspired my sister to be brave, and it was *you* who taught her to be the warrior she is today. So in the end, *you* are the reason for the Revolution, whether you know it or not." He rises to his feet. "The Living despise us, Jennifer. The Living have abused us, too. The Living have taken advantage of the planet. I heard the Whispers that day, same as you. This world is ready to hand itself to the Dead, and Winter is the one who will do it. She fought in battles waged against spider demons, inspired a fiery army that conquered half the Living world, and razed the very place we stand on to its bitter, greedy ground."

I swallow and look away, uncomfortable.

"And when you are ready to join us …" He opens his fingers. The green light from his stone shines. "Just say my name through the stone, and I'll heed your call."

My eyes are drawn to it. "I'm glad I don't remember who Winter is," I admit softly. "She sounds terrifying."

Corpsey's watery eyes linger on my face too long. Then he gives a resigned nod toward a nearby passage. "I'll show you the way out."

Chapter Six

Necrocite

The way out was another winding passage reinforced with wood and rusty metal that ran under the massive, half-fallen walls of the facility and opened to a hidden door in the forest. Corpsey stood silently at that doorway and watched as Grim and I walked off, disappearing into the mist and the twisted, spindly trees.

It's several minutes later that Grim and I, alone now, break the silence. "I feel like I'm escorting a queen."

I'm so distracted with my own thoughts about Mari and John and what my life's become in just a few miserable weeks, I nearly miss what he says. "Huh?"

"There's something truly powerful in you, Jennifer. You have that stone for a reason. I mean, these Undead people think you're here to lead them into war."

I sigh as I step over a large, dead root. "I don't care about whatever they think I'm here for. I just want to find John, seeing as I can't be with my best friend anymore."

"You mean Mari?"

"Who else?" I snap, annoyed. Then: "Sorry."

"It's okay." Grim smiles. "You can yell at me if you want to, if it helps you, if it makes you … feel better. *A bottomless pit down which all fires are forgotten and all embers cool, a song that quiets as it builds, a ribbon of infinite length to bind your ugliest gifts tenfold.* I'll be your friend."

I don't respond to that, or his indulgent poetic prose. Suddenly I find myself wondering how angry Corpsey's sister will be with him when she finds out he let me go.

Sorry about that, Corpsey.

Also: Thank you.

"What was with that 'Green Eye opening' thing you said to your Undead friend?" Grim asks me. "Did you make it up? Or is it something you read in a book?"

"He's not my friend."

"His name is Erick," Grim goes on, "yet you call him Corpsey. I don't think it's common to give a nickname to someone you don't consider a friend."

I stop and turn to Grim. "You're not a friend, yet you give yourself the nickname 'Grim', like some secretive alias. Why do you ask me so many questions?"

He lifts his eyebrows innocently. "I—I don't mean to pry. I'm just … I'm curious about everything to do with the Dead. Like you are. I'm fascinated by it … by *all* of it."

I look over his pale face, his thin figure, his strange obsession.

Winter's Doom

What if there's a reason he stayed so silent around the others? What if Corpsey knows him? What if Grim's a Dead in disguise trying to infiltrate the minds of the Living … using me?

At once, I'm upon Grim, pushing him against a nearby tree with a grunt. "Hey!" he cries out in protest, but I've got a hold of his shirt, right by his neck, and my face is in his, threats in my eyes. "Who are you, really?" I demand of him. "Who are you??"

"Gill McAlister! My real name is Gill! What are you doing?? I'm your friend!"

"Gill??" I give his shirt a shake, then snarl like some wild animal trying to get to the bottom of this. "And who do you work for, *Gill?* Were you sent to spy on me? Do you work for the Dead? *Are you actually one of them??*"

"One of who??" he cries out, nearly in tears.

And that's when I notice the pulse in his neck.

Throbbing … throbbing … throbbing.

Even my fingers against his chest feel it, still gripping a big handful of his shirt—the terrified racing of his heart.

Okay, maybe I'm losing my mind a little.

I let go of him, and this time I can't even bear to say sorry. I just huff and continue walking. After some time, I hear Grim slowly following behind me, and perhaps now he is considerably less inspired to ask any more questions.

The crunching of twigs and dead grass beneath our feet is all we listen to for a very long time.

It might be twenty whole minutes of walking through dead woods when I finally make an observation, speaking glumly. "They already seem so much more … *human* … than they were last time I was here."

Grim is quick to respond, as if eager for us to be on good, comfortable terms again. "Yeah?"

"They seemed so … animalistic before. Feral. They rarely used names for each other. They were also of a fewer number."

"That girl *did* say they're waking up. Ten thousand."

"Ten thousand." I shudder. *I had forgotten the number.* "That's ten thousand too many, if you ask me."

Grim doesn't respond to that.

My hand is in my pocket again, fidgeting with the stone as we walk along. I find I'm less inclined to pull it out, now that I realize Corpsey can see me through it.

What all has he seen, anyway? How many times have I pulled it out of my pocket and stared at it? Did he see me in my condominium on campus? Did he see me while I was at my father's funeral, out in the countryside? Did he see my mother? Did he see John? Did he see Professor Praun when the man returned it to me in my prison cell?

"The Green Eye opens …" I recite out loud, stop, then reluctantly let out the rest: "… when … the Yellow closes. The White has arrived."

"What's that?"

"I didn't tell them *all* the words."

"I don't follow. What words?"

For the sheer lack of having anyone else nearby *who's alive* to share the strange message with, I figure maybe it would be helpful for Grim to know. In fact, considering his poetry-trained mind, he may be able to see something else in the words that I can't.

"Professor Praun visited me secretly in my cell before my trial," I explain. "He urgently told me I needed to relay a message, and ... that was the message."

"*The Green Eye opens when the Yellow closes ...?*"

"*The White has arrived*. Yes. Those are the words."

"Strange. Maybe it's something Professor Praun read in a book. Everything comes from books. I mean, he *is* one of your direct superiors, being head of the history department and all. He has access to *all* the books, even the ones they don't put in the libraries. *The Green Eye opens when* ... Well, we've seen the Green Eye, obviously, but what's the Yellow Eye?"

"I have no idea. And what's this rock in my pocket?" I throw in rhetorically.

"I don't know. But it raises the Dead, clearly."

I eye him. "We don't know that."

"And it has *some* kind of connection with the Green Eye," Grim points out, "since your friend could see you through it."

"Again, not my friend."

"All I know is, I think that rock of yours is going to give you leverage at some point. Maybe it's another Eye that just isn't glowing yet. Oh, if only I've read a poem about *glowing eyes*, I might be of more help. *The Green Eye opens ... Yellow ... The White has arrived ...*" Then he stops. "White." He looks at me. "Are *you* the 'White'?"

I stare at him. "What?"

"Your hair. Your white hair. I mean, I don't mean to be rude, but your hair isn't ... usual ... and you've ... well, you've recently *arrived* in this land. You're here now. And maybe—"

"That's absurd. I can't be part of the message. Then Professor Praun would have said that directly, or he'd have said, '*Winter has arrived*' ... not '*The White*'."

"Hmm." Grim lifts a hand to his chin and drums his fingers along it, working it over. "Hmm," he keeps saying, glancing here and there, thinking.

I touch the rock in my pocket again, bothered. *If this really is another Eye, then why doesn't it glow?*

"Figuring this out is giving me a headache," he says with a grimace. "Or perhaps it's that we haven't eaten or had anything to drink for hours. Hey, do you want to maybe stop in that clearing up ahead for a little rest?"

"And what do you propose we do?" I ask, losing my patience yet again. "Have lunch? Cups of tea? Or should I remind you that *nothing* edible grows on these trees, and Corpsey's sister is going to send an *army of ten thousand Dead* after me when she finds out I'm gone—which she likely knows by now? I'm certain that army is already well on its way in our general direction." I shoot him a look. "Feel like stopping for a *rest* anymore?"

Grim bites his lip, then shakes his head.

Then I continue onward and break through the trees.

And I stop at the edge of the very clearing to which he just referred.

I'm paralyzed to the spot.

"See? It's a … *huge* clearing," points out Grim. "A nice break from the woods, but … yeah, maybe a bad idea to stop. We should just head on across."

The trees stop in a perfect line, as if literally incapable of growing beyond where our feet stand, and for nearly half a mile ahead of us, there is a great, dusty clearing of nothing but dry, cracked dirt and eeriness, which extends on and on to the east and west. Far across the clearing, another line of trees indicate where the forest resumes.

"What is it?" asks Grim, noting my frozen face.

"The Whispers," I answer simply. "This is it."

Grim blinks, staring out at the wastes. "R-Really?"

I peer over my shoulder into the dark woods behind us, seeing nothing, then stare ahead at the greyish expanse. Then something else occurs to me. "Wait. How are we even here? From what Corpsey said the last time I was in this land, no Living can find the Whispers."

"Maybe it's that creepy rock of yours," suggests Grim. "It's clearly some kind of ... Undead artifact or something, so maybe it's our way in."

"We don't want to be *in*. This place is ... vile and ... and *evil*, but ..."

"So why don't we go around it? Avoid it altogether?"

I gaze toward the east, then the west. My eyes narrow with annoyance as I realize there's no easy way around this land-blasted waste. The city of After's Hold is almost an hour walk to the north beyond the Whispers, and if there *is* an end to the Whispers somewhere to the east or west, it's so far away that it would probably take half a day or more just to get around it.

It's like the Whispers is daring me to cross it.

A greedy bridge troll in the shape of grey dust and spookiness and nothing at all.

"We're going to make straight for the forest ahead," I declare darkly, "and we won't stop, hesitate, or change direction no matter what. We can't get lost in there."

"Lost? How would we get lost? I can see clearly from this side to the other."

"Don't let the Whispers deceive you. If it's in one of its *moods*, you'll be swallowed in fog so thick, you can't even see your own hands."

Winter's Doom

Grim studies the side of my face, concerned. "You're speaking of it like it's a person."

"It is." I grit my teeth. "Six *persons*, in fact. Two green children, two yellow men in armor, and two old people with white clouds for legs. I hope never to see the faces of any of them again."

"Hmm. *The Green Eye opens when the Yellow* ... Oh, do you think the words are related to them? Same colors."

I'd thought of that. But standing on the edge of the Whispers with the Dead at my back, I have no time to ponder it now. "All I know is that there are Living on the other side of this wasteland, and we need to get there."

Grim takes a step forward, rubs his foot into the dust, then shrugs. "Seems safe to me."

"Keep at my side. I have a suspicion the Whispers won't take kindly to two Living walking unaccompanied through them." I pull the stone out of my pocket, then grip it tightly. "Better to keep this close, I guess."

Suddenly, Grim seems less sure than he was a second ago. "On second thought, we could go back, join Corpse-guy and his sister, and maybe use their army to find your friend? That sounds rather safer to me."

"And suicidal for my friend. Suck it up, Grim. We're braving the Whispers alone."

With that, I grip my rock and advance into the dusty expanse.

Grim stays at my side, keeping right up with me as he looks in all directions, as if expecting something to pop up at once from the ground, or fall from the thick fog above. I just keep my eyes trained ahead at the forest on the other side, my destination.

It isn't long before I start to feel the slightest pull of wind in my hair.

I ignore it.

The wind picks up more, stirring the loose silt off the ground, forming puffs of dust and fog.

I pick up my pace, hurrying on.

Grim starts walking faster, too, keeping up with me. "J-Jennifer? Is it happening? Are they coming?"

"Don't talk. Just move."

A gust brushes past me with such strength, all my hair is blown into my face. I run a hand through my hair, drawing it all back, and suddenly I can't see the woods at the other end of the Whispers. The dust and the mist has taken it from view.

"J-Jennifer?"

"Keep moving!" I shout back at him.

And suddenly we're running.

I should have known better. I shouldn't have tried to brave the Whispers.

A crack in the ground takes my foot, and I go falling forward, my hands flying out to catch myself.

And my rock flies out of my palm, freed, tumbling into the roiling mist.

"THE STONE!" I cry out.

"I've got it!" cries Grim, racing ahead. "I won't let it get away! I'll get it for you, Jennifer!"

And the fog swallows him, too.

"GRIM!" I climb to my feet and hurry forward, trying not to limp, despite the scrape the fall gave to my knee, and something else that stings on my ankle.

The churning winds are very loud now, intensifying so much, I have to squint against the already blinding fog. *"Grim!"* I shout feebly into the mist. *"Grim! Where are you? Grim!! Shout back at me!!"*

But nothing shouts back. There is only the screaming of deathly winds as they spiral all around me, tossing up my hair and the sleeves of my grey shirt and my flapping, billowing grey pants.

Don't stop. Just keep running. Make it to the trees.

I stare ahead as I throw my feet, eyes squinting against the furious mist, and wait for my next step to break me through the fog at last where I'll see Grim holding my stone, waiting for me by the trees.

And then, almost too quickly, I burst through the fog and head straight for a tree, my hands coming up to stop my face from crashing into it.

I look around, desperate. "Grim!!"

I turn around, peering back into the mist. I look to the left, then the right, then back into the woods. "Grim!!"

He's gone.

I'm all alone.

This is my worst nightmare.

I turn back to face the Whispers, watching the mists as they play and wrestle and fight one another, twisting and writhing like grey-white, wispy snakes. I anxiously wait for the shape of Grim to emerge, hugging the tree as if it keeps me standing, my heart pounding in my ears.

Then I see a dark shape.

"Grim!!" I call out, letting go of the tree to approach the mist.

Until the shape turns into something else.

It's a Dead. *"Wiiinter!"* it moans, reaching its skinless, bony hands toward me.

I back away, horrified.

More shapes appear in the mist. *"Wiiinter!"* they call out. *"Wiiinter! Wiiinter!"* Some of them stumble out of the mist on shaky, limp feet. Others break their way out of the ground, just like they did beneath the rice silo. Some crawl, digging their fingers into the dirt and dragging their legless torsos toward me. *"Wiiinter!"*

Grim is lost. My stone is lost.

I have no choice but to run.

"Wiiinter! Wiiinter!"

Winter's Doom

I tear into the woods, throwing all the moans and cries of my non-name behind me.

Darkness surrounds me again. Trees in all directions. Trees twice as tall as the ones on the other side of the Whispers. With it being so dark, I can barely see five feet ahead of me, and every tree rushing toward my face is a surprise.

At once, the trees open up, and I come to an abrupt stop. I stand at a dried-up riverbank, which cuts through the woods like a shallow trench. Just a shallow foot of water remains in the bottom of the bank, murky and dark.

Is this the same river that John and I encountered last time, the one that guards After's Hold from the water-sensitive Dead who try to cross it?

I hear the stirring of mud and the cracking of branches underfoot. From the ground behind me, I watch the Dead break free.

"Wiiinter!" cries the nearest one.

I back away from it, eyes wide, only to find a hand suddenly gripping my ankle from behind. I let out a shriek and back the other way, but the hand has grabbed me so tightly, I fall.

"Wiiinter!" moans the head of the one who grabbed me as it pushes out of the mud.

"MY NAME ISN'T WINTER!" I scream, then give the head a swift kick with my heel.

The head separates from the body at once and goes flying into the woods, punted like a toy ball. *"I forgiiive youuu!"* shouts the head as it soars through the air. Where it lands, I'll never know.

The moment I'm back on my feet, a set of hands wrap around my body and pull me back against it, like a clumsy hug—and into my ear, a Dead's throaty voice murmurs, *"Ooh, Wiiinter, how I've missed you sooo!"*

"Jennifer! Duck!" comes another voice.

Wait. Is that—? Without hesitation, I duck.

And over my head zips an arrow, which goes straight through the Dead's forehead, pinning him awkwardly to a tree at our backs and setting me free.

"Run, Jennifer! Across the river, to me, run, run!"

I charge for the river just as another arrow goes zipping past my face and lodging itself into another pursuing Dead, causing him (or her?) to fling backwards with a grunt. *"It's okaaay!"* the Dead insists from the ground, awkwardly trying to pull the arrow out of its bony neck. *"I've suffered wooorse wounds for you, Wiiinter, and I'll suffer mooore! Wiiinter!"*

I hop right over the foot of water that remains of the river, then scramble up the opposite end of the bank toward the voice. Another arrow flies over my head, and I keep racing toward the trees, searching.

And then I see him.

Winter's Doom

"J-John?" I gasp, wide-eyed.

Armed with a bow and a quiver of arrows slung over his back, he rushes to my side. "Behind me." He nocks another arrow, aims, then lets it loose. I don't see where it lands—*or in whom*—as I hurry behind him and stare over his shoulder at our pursuers.

All I see are the usual shapes of tall, skeletal trees.

Until I realize half of them are moving toward us.

"Run, Jen," John commands me as he nocks another arrow, then sends it flying. One of the moving trees falls. He nocks another. "I'll be behind you. After's Hold is up through the trees, ten minutes or so, go!"

"It's farther than that, isn't it? We need to run, both of us, John. And Grim is lost in the—There's too many—"

"Go, Jen!"

"I'm not leaving you!"

The Dead are gathering upon us. I don't have the stone anymore. Grim is gone. Corpsey and his sister are somewhere in that mass of Dead, I'm certain, pushing the whole lot of them our way like a rising tide.

"There's no use trying to shoot them all down," I tell him quickly. "We'll both run. Together."

With a glance through the dark at the pursuing Dead, John lets out a growl of frustration, lets loose one last arrow, then nods, relenting. "Alright, let's move."

And move, we do.

John and I rush through the woods, racing away from the Dead who stagger toward us, grunting and moaning and calling out, *"Wiiinter! Wiiinter! Welcome baaack!"* over and over—a whole off-putting sea of Dead men's voices, women's voices, children's voices …

Talk about one disconcerting homecoming.

After a while, the Dead fall far enough behind us that I don't hear them anymore. The only thing filling my ears is the sound of John and I panting as we run, and the dead grass and dirt we're kicking up.

It's then that our running slows, and we stop by a thicket of dry, thorny bushes to catch our breath.

I give his face an honest look for the first time since we reunited. "John."

"Where did they drop you?" he asks first.

"The beach. You?"

"Mouth of the river, near the coast. I followed it up and made my way to After's Hold. It's dried up now, the most of it."

"I noticed."

He takes my hand and pulls me against him, hugging me close. "I worried about you, Jen. I thought they put us into different hovercrafts for a reason. I thought they were going to do away with you, or send you somewhere else, or—"

"I'm here, John. I'm still alive."

Winter's Doom

"Me too." He kisses me right then, and my arms find their way around him, ever grateful to have him here with me despite all else.

My fingers catch on the quiver around his back. "I didn't know you were such a huntsman."

The corner of his lips curl. "I've got a lot of special talents you don't know about."

I bring my lips to his again.

Suddenly he pulls back, a look on his face. "You started to say something about … a 'Grim' being lost …?"

The whole thing strikes me anew. "Grim. He was with me. We found each other after we were dropped. He was with me in the Whispers, and …" I peer over my shoulder into the darkness. "Who knows where he is now. They probably took him."

"Grim …" Then John's face hardens. "You mean that guy who was making a speech at the fountains?" He goes from zero to furious in seconds. "He's the reason we're even here at all, Jennifer. He incited the rioting and the protesting on campus. *It's that bastard's fault we're here!*"

My eyes grow wide. "John," I chide him.

"And he was with you?" A growl escapes his throat. "If I see that pretentious poet, I'll beat him down. And if any harm comes to you while we're here, Jennifer, I won't let him survive whatever my fists do to his face."

"John, stop."

There's a snap of a twig somewhere in the woods. John and I glance outward, eyes wide, looking for the noise. Nothing stirs.

"We need to get to the city," he whispers.

"Good idea."

The pair of us hurry past the thicket, careening with urgency through the trees.

We don't stop again.

Nor do we discuss the ever-touchy subject of Grim.

The walls of After's Hold are exactly as I remember them: tall, cold, and made of thick metal, and they appear so abruptly that their presence startles me. "Up, up!" calls John to an unseen someone, and at once, the walls before us—which are actually the smooth, metal gates of the city—slowly part to let us in. They shut at our backs, and at once, I feel my first scrap of safety and security since I was dumped on that vile beach.

"Are you hurt?"

I look up into John's face. "No. You?"

"I'm safe. I spoke with the Mayor earlier, who … isn't quite over her grudge with us. She wanted to keep the 'savage boy' in her custody to try and … reform him, or something. Instead, we released him and used him to get us into the Whispers. She didn't care for our reasoning."

When the Mayor captured Corpsey, she called him 'the savage boy'. Their blood-hungry kind aren't exactly welcomed here in After's Hold, even if the Mayor has a soft spot for them. "Well, she's going to have to forgive us. It was necessary we went there … even if the burden of what I learned is too much to bear."

John's eyes glaze over.

Oh. I forgot this is a sore subject between us.

"You … still refuse to tell me what happened that day," he says, his voice quiet, small. "In the Whispers."

I close my eyes, freshly traumatized by the place from having just walked through it and experienced its furious mists all over again. Grim … The stone …

And maybe the last thing I need my boyfriend to know is that his girlfriend is the cause of the end of the world.

Can't I just be his Jennifer? And he, my John?

"Did Grim do anything to you?" he asks suddenly.

My eyes flick to him. "What do you mean?"

"Did he try to harm you? Did he ask you anything strange? You said he was with you in the Whispers, just now. You had to cross the Whispers to get here, right?"

I nod. "And it was just as terrifying as it was the first time. But I lost Grim in the Whispers, and—"

"I don't trust him."

I sigh. "You don't *know* him."

"He's a worm with an agenda."

"We need to speak with the Mayor," I state, shifting the topic abruptly, "because we're running out of time the longer we sit here and debate about some *poet*. A whole army of the Dead is waking up right now. I've seen them climb straight out of the ground, dozens, hundreds of them. I don't know why. I think it's because of me."

John squints. "Because … of you?"

"Yeah, me. And there's, like, ten thousand of them."

John's eyes go wide. He says nothing.

"The Mayor needs to secure the city," I tell him. "We need … We need weapons, or something. I don't know. I'm not an expert in wars and sieges and strategies. All I know is, Corpsey and his bald, one-eyed sister, they're heading here with a very, very large army of Dead."

"We're safe here," John insists at once. "The walls of After's Hold are made of steel. *Their* kind of Dead can't come in, nor climb in, since they can't touch the metal without frying like morning bacon."

I wince, gripping my stomach. "Really, did you *have* to mention morning bacon?"

"Oh, I'm sorry, Jen." He puts an arm around me, then starts to walk me down the road. "Come on, I'll take you to our Retreat. We can forget everything else until we've gotten you some refreshments."

What a hilarious notion.

Refreshments, in a world like this.

"Thank you," I murmur to him anyway, then cling to his side as we walk.

Winter's Doom

He guides me past the tall buildings, and I listen to the eerie noise they make when the wind blows through their broken windows and snakes into their hollowed bodies. In many of those windows, I see people peering out at me, though once again, I can't tell who's Living or Dead.

"There are more people here," I note.

"Many other Living found this place over the past week, so I've heard. Not to mention all of those who were just dumped here recently by the hovercrafts, along with you and me. The number of us almost match the number of Dead at this point."

"Wow. More of us finding this place and surviving? That's great news."

"It'd be better news if it didn't mean twice as many mouths to feed," John points out.

I deflate.

When we reach Winter's Retreat—the apartment building in which John, Connor, Dana, and I stayed the last time we were all here together—all of those familiar feelings of dread flood my system from the first time we were here. I feel the worry and pain of not knowing what to do next. I feel anxiety as fresh as if I had just come here for the first time, except now it feels twenty times worse. This time, I don't have the extra benefit of comfort in thinking that my human comrades at the university might soon come and rescue me.

They are the ones who banished me here.

"Don't be alarmed," John warns me, "by what you're about to see."

I flash him a look of concern. "What's that?"

When we enter the doors of Winter's Retreat, I find a long line of several people, which ends at the door to one of the first-floor apartments—or perhaps it's an office, I can't tell from here. The thing with the citizens of After's Hold is that you don't know which are Living and which are Dead; the Dead here fix themselves up properly and maintain their appearance, much like the Beautiful Dead who I researched all about. So as I gaze upon this spread of people, I realize I don't know whose hearts are beating and whose hearts don't.

As John takes me ahead of the line, I notice eyes start to find mine, and many of them go wide with surprise. One woman I don't know waves excitedly at me. Another gasps and nudges her friend, who then also takes to staring at me in awe. *"Jennifer-Winter!"* hisses another one of them, then wiggles her fingers in my direction.

Then I hear her voice from within the room where the front of the line leads: "Oh, oh, *yes*, I *do* see a great and *exciting* journey in your future, *yes, I do! It's in the cards!*"

I stop in place the moment I'm in the room—an office with a desk, a wide window at the back, and a dead potted plant. "Dana??" I cry out.

Winter's Doom

Dana the Diviner—still very much alive—looks up from the cards she has spread out upon the desk. A couple of ladies sit in front of her, apparently having their futures being read, and they turn to shoot me a pair of annoyed looks at having their reading be interrupted.

Dana rises at once. "Oh, Jennifer, my love, my sweet! You're back!"

She is every bit of the Diviner she was before. Her hair is a giant, matted bush of insanity. Her arms are long and skinny and dressed with countless bands and bracelets. She is adorned in a silken gown that has seen far better days—and a pair of tattered leather shoes she tries to hide underneath it.

"And you've survived a week in this place." I smile at the woman. "I'm still so shocked you chose to stay behind when they came to rescue us."

A dark look takes over her face. She purses her lips, then lifts a papery finger. "Well, after I learned the *heinous* way in which C and her friends were treated …" Dana lets out a scandalized huff, then dismisses her anger with a sweep of her hand in the air. "Let it suffice to say, I was much obliged *not* to have a thing to do with the Living again. *This* is my home now."

"C?" I ask, not recognizing the name. "Who is C?"

"You might remember her as the rude one with the two friends who threatened us to stay away from their building. She has a violin, remember? I've gotten to know everyone in town, what with my new fortunetelling business and—Oh, listen to me, going on. John's told me the ugly turn of events in the world of the Living. How they used me for blame, then turned around and blamed all of you anyway. Such deceivers, the Living! I feel as if I'm not one anymore, the way they've betrayed me!—if but for my still-filling lungs and still-beating heart. Oh, *you* must be so very absolutely heartbroken, my dear!"

I give her a slow, sad nod. "Especially after the loss of my father, now I've left my mom all alone. Truly alone." A soft smile finds my face. "I thought of you at my dad's funeral."

Dana takes my hands at once, and her eyes harden with warm sincerity. "He misses you, my dear, and he is ever so proud of the … the sheer *bravery* you've shown these past few weeks. Yes, he is."

I stare back into Dana's eyes.

There was a time when her words would have made me furious, bothered me to no end, made me want to burn all the silly soul-reading cards on her desk.

Instead, I find myself rather grateful for the comfort of them, whether it's real or not. "Thank you, Dana."

"And you must *continue* to be brave," Dana then assures me, her eyes hard as a wary mother's. "Especially now. You must be more brave than you've ever been."

Winter's Doom

"Um, excuse me," says one of the women at the desk, taking the hand of her friend in the chair next to her and turning around to face us, "but we were in the middle of a *reading*, which you *interrupted*." "Yeah," throws in the other at me, far less polite. "End of the line is *back there*."

I give them a tired, apologetic smile. "Sorry, I was just reconnecting with my friend Dana here, whom I—"

"JENNIFER STEEL!"

All of us jump in place at the booming sound of the voice that invades the room like a ripple of thunder.

There in the doorway stands a woman so shockingly tall, she can't fit through the door without slouching her head and half her back. Her hair is still a fuzzy white ball, like the end of a cotton swab, and her eyelashes are so long, they are likely to catch flies with every blink.

"Mayor Damnation," I greet her, recognizing the woman at once. "I know you're not pleased with me, but I can explain everything, and I need your help. I just—"

At once, her booming voice is traded for something far more high and melodic: "Hello there, Jenny-thing," she cuts me off. "Isn't it a much cuter way to call you, instead of Jennifer? You've a drab Living name, if you ask me, no offense meant. I have taken after my dear assistant Truce, you might say." She eyes Dana suddenly. "You owe me a reading. I have heard remarkable things this week about your ... *talent* ... for communicating with the deceased-and-not-yet-Raised. Mmm, your connection to the spirit world will be sung about in songs for many long and boring millennia to come."

"Why, thank you!" returns Dana with a sweeping, dramatic bow, taking her words for a great compliment.

The Mayor turns upon me again. Her voice remains sweet as she states, "You and I have unfinished business."

I sigh. "Do we really have to do this? I only *just* had to endure a trial on my side of the ocean. Must we do the same on this side?"

The Mayor doesn't answer, merely turning to leave, the tattered cloak she wears sweeping in her departure, and I'm left with the feeling that I'm expected to follow. John quickly gives me a handful of nuts and some bread off a small cart parked on the side of the room, as well as a glass of water poured from a pitcher. I greedily consume everything that's given to me—much to the watchful chagrin of the two women still waiting for the rest of their fortune, or whatever it is I've interrupted.

"We'll see each other again soon," Dana assures me. "Go handle your business, and I'll finish up here with mine. Now, where were we?" she sings as she takes her place behind the desk again. "Ah, yes. Two of cups, and three of wolves, and the King's Blood. Yes, yes, I *do* see an *adventure* in your future, indeed. Oh, yes, and the sea …"

I don't hear whatever else she sees for them.

Winter's Doom

John and I walk the long path to the office of the Mayor, which is still deep in the heart of an old building I suspect might've been a library or bookkeeping office of some kind. The Mayor sits on the same heap of broken, overturned furniture as she did before, packed with piles of paper, discarded office supplies, shattered glass, copy machines, and tons of books. One such book is in her hand, from which she seems to be lazily reading, her long legs crossed and her lips pursed with mild focus.

Standing at the base of the hoard of trash, I spot the ever-recognizable, colorful, powdery-faced woman called Truce, whose tiny face is crowded by curly yellow strands of maybe-plastic hair. She is Mayor Damn's right hand.

"Hello, Jenny-thing," she greets me, her voice full of airy sugar.

Goodness, I have to deal with two of them calling me that, now? Mayor Damnation is stirred by Truce's greeting, as if she literally didn't hear us enter the room, despite how very well the Dead can hear. "Oh, there you are," mutters the Mayor, then carelessly tosses the book she was reading over a shoulder. It lands with a thud somewhere behind her. "So go ahead and explain yourself. We gave you trust. We left you alone in a cell with the savage boy, with express instructions *not* to open the cage, or even to approach it. And then—"

"I'm sorry, I—"

"—you not only *freed* the boy, but ran away with him and John—the three of you, like three little Heart Beater bandits in the night. Well, *you two* Heart Beaters, not him. John explained to me his side, of course, but he left out one very important piece of the story, which only *you* are able to tell." The tall woman leans forward, which is quite an effect, considering her height, and while batting her big, crimson eyelashes, she asks, "What happened in the Whispers, my sweet Jenny-thing?"

The very thing she wants to know is the one thing I don't want to reveal.

So what do I do? Lie to the woman? Lie to John?

"Really," the Mayor continues flippantly, gesturing in the air with her long fingernails, "I can forgive *absconding* with the savage boy. Honestly, the subject bores me. My interest is in the *Whispers* … which have been altogether silent and asleep for hundreds of long, long years … until, as I understand it, *you* came along."

I let out a petulant sigh. "There's not much to say."

"I think there's *plenty* to say."

I glance at John for support, only to find him staring at me expectantly, waiting on my next words. Yes, even *John* I've kept the secret from. He wants to know just as badly as the Mayor does.

"Mayor Damn, I said earlier that I need your help."

"And I need a story. What happened in the Whispers?"

Winter's Doom

"The ... *savage* Dead are going to try and storm the city. They're after me. They think I've come to lead them into some kind of 'Revolution' to take over the Living world. They keep calling me Winter."

"Of course they do. So tell me what happened in the Whispers."

She simply won't let it go, will she? "This is a far more important—and time-sensitive—matter, Mayor Damn-It. There are ten thousand of them, and my friend Mari is among them."

"What?" interrupts John.

Oh. That part was news to him. "Mari joined them," I tell him, my eyes sad. "She thinks she belongs to them because she doesn't remember me."

"Who is this Mari?" asks the Mayor. "Is she the one for whom you had to go to the Whispers to rescue?"

"Yes, but it turned out that the Dead claimed her that day. She was made Undead, and now she doesn't know who I am."

"Oh. So quickly?" The Mayor purses her lips in that way she does, staring off in thought. "It isn't usually such a quick process, to go from Living to Dead. How *queer*."

"Look, Ma'am Damn," I address her. *Really, I can come up with twenty different names for her.* "I know the walls here are made of steel, but something tells me even *that* obstacle won't hold the savage army back for long."

"So tell me what occurred in the Whispers, then."

"But it's not relevant. I think the *army of ten thousand* at our doorstep is far more important, and we need—"

"The Whispers are just as important. In fact ..." The woman rises from her perch, making her look as tall as a demigod on that mountain of discarded junk. "I suspect the two issues are intimately connected."

That stops me. "Connected?"

"Yes, connected. The issue of the savage army outside our city, and the issue of what you witnessed while in the Whispers. For it wasn't until you invoked the Whispers that the Dead have risen in such numbers. So let's have it, Jenny-thing." She snaps her fingers. "Tell me. My patience is wearing *ice* thin."

I stammer, my gaze flitting from the Mayor, to John, to a squinting, suspicious Truce. "I'm ... I've just ..."

It's John's long, questioning stare that does me in.

I can't continue to lie to him.

There's really no way out of this.

I take a long, deep breath, then let it all out. "The Whispers emerged while I was with the savage boy, whose real name is Erick, although I call him Corpsey. The Whispers said that I resemble something ... *someone* called Winter, and that my existence is a symptom that the end of the world is to come."

The Mayor squints at me. "A symptom?"

"A sign. Something like that." I realize I'm picking at my fingers. I stop and drop my hands to my sides. "I don't know how much of it I believe, or if they are just spiritual bullies trying to scare me."

She wrinkles her face. "Spiritual ... bullies?"

"And before they faded away, they told me a few last words ... and I repeated the words to the 'savage Dead', and ... it seemed to affect them greatly, because at once the bald one who leads them softened toward me, and suddenly I was a celebrity among them ... just seconds before we were rescued and taken home. 'You did this to yourself. The only one left to blame is you.' I even remember the words."

"I have no idea what that means," mutters the Mayor in a tone that suggests equal parts fascination and equal parts utter boredom.

"And now that I'm back," I go on, letting the flood gates flow, "they're treating me like a goddess. Not to mention Grim, a Living guy I was banished here with, who seems to think I'm capable of Raising the Dead with a stone I have. *Had*," I amend with a frustrated huff.

It's then that John says, "Stone?"

I turn to him. The sound of his voice reflects every bit of emotion inside him—the surprise at how much I've kept from him, the dark content of my secrets—and now the news that I'd brought our one prized possession here.

And lost it. "Yes. Our stone. I lost it when I crossed the Whispers. It fell from my hands."

John looks hurt. "You … You lost it?"

I sigh. "John, it was *madness* in there. It was like … like the Whispers wanted to *take* it from me."

Truce stirs from her spot, reminding us all that she's still there. "What is this *stone*, exactly?" she asks.

"I don't know what it is," I admit. "It's dark, heavier than it looks like it ought to be, and kills things it gets near. It's from the Living side of the ocean."

The Mayor scrambles down her hoard—setting loose small trinkets and bits of wood tumbling down the pile—and puts herself right in front of me, her eyes wide and fierce. "Is it black, this stone? Impossibly black? So dark, you're sure no light could possibly color it? And cold to the touch, like ice? And as dense as a troubled soul?"

I'm stunned by the sudden accuracy. "Y-Yes," I admit, staring at her blankly. "How'd you—?"

"Necrocite," she states.

Truce gasps at the Mayor's word, slapping a hand to her own mouth. All of us turn to look at her, alarmed by her reaction. "Oh," Truce murmurs after a moment, then drops her hand. "What a … What an unlovely word. I don't much like that word at all. I'd much rather find a more fitting word. Such as: dull, nothing, unimportant rock. Do not speak of that rock again. It makes me feel so very sad. And angry. And I'd much rather like to not feel either of those emotions."

"Truce, are you alright?" I ask softly.

Quite suddenly, Truce turns and departs the room, the clicking of her heels echoing as she heads down the long hall of the building, vanishing.

The Mayor sighs, then plops her butt down on the edge of a nearby overturned desk. "Well, I suppose it might make sense, why the Dead are so drawn to you."

I frown. "Necrocite? Is that what my stone was?"

"Seems to be." She pinches the bridge of her nose, as if nursing an oncoming headache. "It's an ancient material that no soul has seen in this land for a very long time. Much like the green warlock stones, of course. I wouldn't worry. Without one, there is no fear of the other."

I bite my lip, then cast my eyes to the floor, worried.

John notices. "Jen …?"

I turn my stony eyes onto him. "Corpsey has one."

"Has what?" asks the Mayor, eyeing me.

"A green stone. It glows. He showed me."

If the Mayor was pretending to breathe this whole time, she at once forgets to, for every muscle in her body turns perfectly rigid in that instant, and her eyes look as if they have converted into solid glass.

I don't much like the look of her paralyzed shock at all. "M-Mayor?"

"So it's happening." The Mayor falls back suddenly with a papery thud, like a child flipping backwards onto a mattress, except her peculiar bed is made of paper, books, and broken furniture. "The Undeathly Revolution. Oh, I thought I'd never see the day. Winter has arrived."

Of all the things she's said in this exchange, those words scare me the worst. I hear Praun's echoing voice in my small cell all over again: *The White has arrived …*

I come around the desk and stand over her body. "Mayor, do you know something? About the stones? And this so-called Revolution? What is happening, exactly?"

"You should join them," the Mayor announces to the ceiling at once. "Yes, I think that's most wise."

John and I share a baffled look before turning our eyes back onto her. "Join them??" the both of us retort.

"You want to get back home, don't you? Well, the Dead are now motivated more than ever to cross that sea. They will find a way. Perhaps you ought to not burn all your bridges and close all your doors. You may need one of them to get home. There are Other Living here, too, you know, and they might depend on you keeping a bridge or two intact for them."

"I-I'm *not* aiding Corpsey and his sister in their wild, reckless, world-ending agenda," I argue back.

"Your Human friends here are starving, Jenny-thing." The Mayor continues to speak to the ceiling, her voice far away, faint, and dreamy. "Think of them. Think of home. Think of your soothsayer friend Dana."

"Mayor, they want to bring about the end of the world as we know it. I *am* thinking of the Living when I resist the savage boy and his sister. *Ugh, now* I'm *calling them savage*," I add under my breath.

The Mayor sits up at once and takes my hands. Her skin is papery and cold. "Trust me, my sweet little Living. I've existed far longer on this immortal plane than you have. Their war is inconsequential. What matters more is that you use the opportunities given to you. Try to see these savage people with an open heart. Once you get back to the land of the Living, you'll have a chance—revered as you are by them—to change their ways." She smiles. "Maybe they are more like us than we know."

"You still have your soft spot for them," I note.

"Oh, is that what Truce called it?" The Mayor lets out a wormy little giggle, then inspects her fingernails. "I've grown weary of this side of the sea. Make friends with the savage, will you? It may be your only chance of survival."

At once, the doors to the building burst open, and in comes Truce, her yellow curls disheveled and her eyes wide with terror. "The Savage have breached the city!!" she cries, hands slapped to her face. "They're burrowing straight out of the ground, hundreds of them!"

Chapter Seven

So Much Dead

We rush out of the Mayor's building to find the streets overrun by Dead and the ground pocked with countless holes where they've climbed out.

Well, if this isn't the definition of a nightmare, I don't know what is.

"Jen, what's happening?" breathes John.

"Exactly what happened in the Whispers. And before that in the Necropolis." I put myself behind John at once, shielding my face. "You need to hide me. If they see me, they'll start doing that *thing* again."

"What thing?" asks John.

The Mayor, her hearing perfect, flicks her eyes upon the two of us. "There's no hiding that white hair of yours, Jenny-thing. Remember my words. Find their leader."

Then I catch eyes with a Dead, who gasps at the sight of me and cries, *"Wiiinter!"* Another hears the name and spots me, too. *"Winter! Winter!"*

I frown. *"That* thing," I answer John belatedly.

Winter's Doom

As if part of one mind, both John and I break into a sprint, racing down the street and dodging the pursuing Dead as they attempt to surround us. We turn the corner and run down a street not yet flooded by them, which in turn leads us straight to Winter's Retreat.

But upon our arrival, we find Dana and several of her patients scurrying out of the building, pouring into the front courtyard. "Oh, oh, Dead, so much Dead!" sings Dana, panicked. "All of them coming out of the ground! What's going on? Is this whole city built upon an ancient graveyard?"

"It's likely safe to assume the entire *continent* is built on a graveyard," I throw back, then grip Dana by the shoulders. "We've got to run, or else find a very smart place to hide. The Dead—"

"I've got a place."

John, Dana, and I turn toward the voice. It comes from a slim young woman with mahogany skin, choppy hair, and a knife clutched in her fist. We met the last time I was here, and she wanted nothing to do with me.

And now she's got a place.

"C, oh, thank the spirits! Take us there!" begs Dana, then beckons me along as she rushes away with the woman named C down an alley.

John and I hurry along into the dark between two buildings. It winds through a series of back alleyways behind Winter's Retreat, which lead us to a greenhouse built into the back of a building, with the street nowhere in sight. "In," directs C coolly as she holds open the glass door, and the three of us hurry inside.

Despite it being a greenhouse with glass walls, there are vines that run up the walls, shielding us from view. Growing on them are fruits and vegetables, which catch me by surprise. "Has this always been here?" I ask. "Why didn't we know about this before?"

"Because I didn't trust you before," answers C in her cool, clipped tone. She comes to a stop by one of the tables and faces us. "But circumstances have changed."

"Why do you trust me now?" I ask her, suspicious. "I seem to recall you threatening to turn my hair into new bow strings for your violin."

"Because now, we've been put here by the same hand of justice," she answers. "Same as Andie. Same as Todd."

And by her words, two emerge from an open door behind her leading into the building: first, a giant of a man with muscles that look angry, dark hair to his shoulders, a face that looks like it has exactly one thought a minute, and whose skin is a golden russet color, and secondly, a boy of maybe twelve years with hair the red-orange color of the sun as it rises, a freckled, rosy complexion with a sickly, yellowish undertone, and whose body is so thin and malnourished, I worry for his health.

Winter's Doom

I recognize them as the other two who accompanied C the first time I met her. "Andie," I address the younger boy, making a guess, "and ... Todd?" I address the giant.

Neither of them confirm my guesses, the two standing silently in the back of the room, staring dully back.

I'll just assume I'm right.

"I suffered an unfair trial, much like yours," says C, "except I was entirely innocent of my crimes. The murder of two government officials, pinned on me. I declared my innocence with more evidence than necessary to prove it, and still I was sentenced to sixty years. Even my mother was convinced to testify against me. I may never know what they have over her, if anything at all but threats and power. Of course, I didn't spend a day in their prison. I was shipped directly here. That was seven years ago."

I gasp. "Seven years?? You've been surviving here for seven years??"

"Indeed, she has," cuts in Dana, nearly giddy.

I shake my head, amazed and hurt. "I'm so sorry, C."

"I'm not. It helped me see the world for the way it is, rather than the way I want it to be." She looks at me. "And I've learned many things over the years ... like the nature of that necrocite you lost in the Whispers."

Wait. How does she know—?

"So are you going to join them?" C then asks. "The Dead we call the Savage? Or have you yet to decide?"

I part my lips, struck by her question. "I … How—?"

"I overheard what the Mayor said to you. Your whole discussion before the Savage breached the city." C smirks knowingly and picks at her fingers. "I'm skilled at getting where I'm not supposed to be without anyone becoming aware, Living *or* Dead. How do you think I've survived this long? Then after the Savage Dead invaded the city, I ran along behind you, unseen, following you all the way back to your Retreat, and now here we stand." She lifts an eyebrow. "And I heard the Mayor's suggestion for you to join the Savage cause. So will you?"

"Of *course* she won't," blurts John on my behalf, his tone sharp. "Whose side do you think she's on?"

I look at him. "But Mayor Damn pointed out that I could use them to my advantage. You know … to find a way back home."

John stares at me as if I've just turned into a giant talking tarantula. "Jennifer … You can't be serious. Why should we bother trying to get back home, anyway? They've made outlaws of us. They don't want us there."

"So? We can live as outlaws then," I retort. "Once the Dead get us back home, they can have the university and our selfish, deceitful government. I'll find my mother, and all of us Living can escape to the countryside where they will never touch us. Dana, you can come, too."

"Oh …" Dana's eyes go wide, uncertain, scared.

Winter's Doom

"And you, too," I say to C. "And you, Todd, and you, Andie—assuming I'm addressing the right one of you by the right name. We can all go there and start over. Anew. No rules or laws or banishments."

"While the Dead slowly eat away at our world? Jen." John puts his face right in front of mine and lowers his voice to something between tense and angry. "The Dead can't be trusted, no matter how *friendly* they seem. They are eternal beings; *we* are not. They have *no* stake in the survival of this planet; *we do*. After we die, what'll they do with the world we've left behind? Your countryside will look as dead as the Whispers. They can't even walk across grass without each and every blade of it shriveling away from them and dying. This world and all of the Life on it needs to be *protected* from them, not *given* to them."

"We're not talking *giving* the world to them," I argue back, frustrated. "We're talking *sharing*, John."

"Sharing?" John lets out one bark of exasperated laughter. "You seriously think that *Army of Savage Dead* your former best friend Mari just joined are interested in *sharing* this planet? That bald, one-eyed woman and her creep of a brother? The same ones who tried to eat your face off the first time they met you?"

"I ..." My heart fills with doubt. "I don't know. I—"

"We're not giving them our planet, Jen. Not today. Not ever."

Silence falls over the greenhouse as I close my eyes, John's words echoing in my ears and crushing my spirit. *Not today. Not ever.* I don't even hear the Dead outside, nor the crying out of that word that *isn't* my name.

"If you want to regain your upper hand," C tells me, "you need to get that necrocite back."

I open my eyes. "What do you know about it? *How* do you know about it?"

C shrugs. "I read all about it in an abandoned library deeper inland where the grass still grows, except they also called the necrocite by ten other names. It's basically catnip to the Dead. Do you like cats? I don't. If you hold a piece of necrocite in your hand, you can control the Dead. They'll obey you. They'll do nearly anything for someone in command of a piece of necrocite. You can convince the Dead to end their war on the Living, if you wanted."

"But I had the stone when I first got here," I point out, "and I couldn't do any of those things. I felt like I had no power over it at all."

"Maybe you were using it wrong." C peeks through the glass wall, then glances back at me. "Needless to say, you need to get it back. And quickly. Because the Dead are gaining in strength—and number."

"No. I'm *not* going back to the Whispers. That piece of necrocite is as good as lost."

"And so are we without it."

Winter's Doom

A vibration begins to fill the greenhouse, causing us all to grow still. The pots on the tables stir, trembling ever so slightly, rattling. The vibration deepens as it becomes a rhythm, like marching …

The glass windows start to shudder loudly.

"They're coming," I say without knowing for sure.

C presses her face to the glass. "I don't see them."

Then the table in the middle of the room shakes as the floor breaks apart, and a single arm reaches through.

Dana shrieks and charges out of the greenhouse, bursting through the front glass door, gone. I'm about to call out for her when another arm bursts through the floor, shattering the wooden floorboards at our feet. John and C and the rest of us back away toward the back door to the building as four separate Dead climb out of the floor, grunting and panting as they break free.

And before our eyes, the beautiful vines and plants of the greenhouse slowly shrivel and recoil, turning from a vivid green to sickly shades of yellow, black, and grey as they wither and die.

Without a word, all five of us charge into the building and race through its empty, unlit rooms toward the only source of light: a door that empties to the street.

"We can't go back onto the street!" I cry out. "They're crawling with them! We have to leave the city! They will find us no matter where we hide in this place!"

"This way," commands C, leading us down a dark, narrow hallway and through a side door, which empties to a different alleyway. I grip John's hand as we run, and I throw a hollow wish over my shoulder that Dana doesn't meet her end while running off to wherever she's gone.

C takes us down more winding alleys, which lead to a wide side street where part of the outer wall is crumbled, giving us a path straight out of the city and back into the dark, dead wilderness.

In seconds, we're surrounded by trees, plunging into the darkness once more, unseen.

We don't stop. C keeps running ahead, Andie and Todd flanking her, and I maintain my hold on John's hand as I follow the woman, trusting wherever she leads us.

It's only when we reach the remains of a half-fallen cabin in the woods—which is missing a roof, a door, and two of its four walls—that we come to a stop to catch our breath. Behind one of the two remaining walls, we crouch and stay silent, listening to the dark, waiting to see if any of the Dead caught on to our departure and followed us. C huddles with her friends in the corner while John and I sit some distance away near the end of the wall by a small, crude-looking chair that's missing a leg.

It's such a strange world over here, devoid of insects and birds and things that make noise. Out here, the air is full of a perpetual, lifeless, soundless nothingness.

"You brought the necrocite here," says C after a time.

I turn to her in the corner with her friends. "So?"

"There is none of it here anymore. None of it that's been found, at least." She scratches at a spot on her arm, then looks at me, her eyes heavy and somber. "Perhaps it was kept in the land of the Living for a reason."

"I … wait a second. What are you saying?"

"I'm saying your stone seems to have awakened the Dead. They'd lost hope. Countless of them went into the ground to slumber. Now they are waking." C rises off the dusty, wooden floor and starts slowly pacing. "Your friend Mari joined the Savage Army, I overheard?"

Just the mention of her name hurts. Even now, I find myself hoping she's okay. "Yes … she did."

"You may have lost her to them forever." C shakes her head solemnly, glancing off toward the half-fallen fireplace on the other side of the broken cabin. "The Dead are having less and less Waking Dreams now. They are forgetting themselves … and losing their own humanity. It makes them despise the Living." She stops pacing and looks at me. "Where did you find it in the first place?"

I'm still thinking about Mari. "Find what?"

"Your piece of necrocite. Where did you find it?"

I glance at John before I answer. "It was kept in the university gardens, behind a glass shield in an enclosure."

"Hmm." C frowns and glances off in thought.

Andie whimpers, "I'm hungry." Todd gives the kid a grunt of warning, and Andie shrinks away and hugs his knees, his complaining silenced.

I look at John again. *"Is C saying this is my fault?"* I whisper under my breath.

John puts an arm around me and holds me close to him. *"It'd be my fault, not yours. I'm the one who broke into that glass and took the rock."*

"And I'm the one who brought the cursed thing here." I let out a sigh and fall against John's chest, exhausted. I think all of us are sharing Andie's discomfort of hunger, despite none of us saying it. Those couple bites of nuts and bread I had earlier sure aren't sufficing.

John's lips come close to my ear. *"I'm sorry if I was harsh earlier, Jen. About your wanting to work with the Dead."*

"It's okay."

"This is a nightmare for me. To be back here. I thought we were free from this place forever."

"Me, too. Though ..." With my head still on his chest, I peer out toward the woods, revealed by the missing walls of the cabin. It always feels like nighttime in this world. *"I don't feel as far away from home as I thought I would. I ... I still remember feeling so full of ... of thrill ... of excitement the first time we came here. No matter how scary or dark or dangerous it is ... I feel like a hole in my heart is filled by this place. Is that odd?"* I ask, lifting my head from his chest to see his face.

Winter's Doom

I find him staring at me strangely.

The look in his eyes worry me. *"John?"*

He runs a hand gently through my hair, pulling some strands off my face and tucking them behind my ear. *"Winter white ..."* he murmurs thoughtfully.

"Just kiss me," I beg him, *"and help me feel like I'm home again. Just for a moment."*

John studies my face for a long and pensive moment. Then his lips descend onto mine, and I feel the sweet, swelling safety of his kiss.

I close my eyes, melting into a dream.

I feel perfectly at home. We might as well be cuddled up in our condominium, as long as I keep my eyes closed. It could be any Saturday morning, too early for the sun to be in the sky, nothing but darkness and stars through our tall glass windows. I feel his heartbeat thrum against my fingers that are pressed against his chest, and his breath crashes against my face, warm and strong.

When I ask him to help me feel at home with just a kiss, John Mason sure knows how to deliver.

"What does the C stand for?" asks Andie timidly.

Our kiss ends with that question, as the pair of us glance toward the corner where Andie sits. He's staring at C, who stands a few paces away near the fallen fireplace. She regards him for five long seconds before turning away without a response, staring off toward the woods.

"C for criminal," grunts Todd, and I hear his gruff, throaty voice for the first time. "C for coldhearted."

Andie hugs his knees tighter, then glances off at C himself. "C for ... curious," he murmurs quietly, as if his question was the precursor to some impromptu guessing game. "C for ... compassionate. S-Sometimes," he adds meekly, his voice cracking.

C doesn't respond to any of the guesses, remaining as still and silent as the ruins surrounding her.

"What did they offer you?" asks John suddenly.

For a second, I think he's asking C. When I turn back to him, I find his eyes on mine. "Offer me? To join them? The Dead didn't offer—"

"No. Back home. The Court. When you were tried. What did they offer you to make you confess your crimes and avoid sentencing?"

I'm thrown by his question. "I ... didn't get an offer."

"Of course you did," retorts John, eyebrows pulling together. "I was told you and Mari were given offers. They said if I went on record confessing my involvement with your crimes, I'd only be sentenced to 240 hours of civil labor and would serve no time in prison."

I gawk at him, unsure what to say.

John stares at me in disbelief. "You ... really weren't offered anything? They lied to me?"

I scoff lightly. "Are you really surprised?"

"Well ..." He looks off, seeming at a loss.

I study his face. "But you turned them down ...?"

"Of course I did."

"Why?"

He turns his gaze on me, his eyes looking like two flakes of burning coal. "Jen, I would have had to forever taint your name with the confession and bring shame on you and your family." John shakes his head sternly. "I couldn't do that. I wouldn't. I stood against the Judge and said I would do no such thing."

"John, why did you do that?? You don't deserve to be here. You deserved a life and an education at Skymark. It's all you ever wanted, to become an engineer. And I—"

"You opened my eyes, Jennifer. You made me realize how much bigger the world is. It's bigger than that stuffy campus that rejected me time and again. It's bigger than you or me. It's even bigger than life and death itself."

I don't know what to say to that, my stunned gaze lost in John's impassioned one.

Andie makes a strange squeaking sound, drawing all our attention. "Y-You're both from Skymark University?"

John and I share a look, then nod.

"Oh." The boy shrinks away, looking miserable.

I'm not sure what to make of that until C suddenly volunteers an explanation: "His mother is the president of that corrupt, treacherous place."

I do a double-take at the boy. His reddish orange hair. His freckles. "You're … Rosella Vale's son …??"

"He is," answers C on his behalf. "Andie Vale, sitting before you. The president's ex-husband—Andie's father—betrayed their secret knowledge of the Dead's existence to a colleague. President Vale, feeling threatened, pulled a few of her government influence strings and got her ex-husband jailed indefinitely. Andie, disillusioned with how evil his own mother had become, sided with his dad. The price for that was being cast away to the Sunless Reach."

"What a horrible thing to do," I say through a gasp, a hand to my cheek. "And to her own son!"

"Maybe our government deserves the Savage Dead." C returns to Andie's side and puts a gentle palm on his cheek, caressing it like a mother. "He's been safe with us since his exile a year ago. We look after each other, don't we?" Andie gives her a weak, doleful smile.

My fingers clench into fists, just thinking of that pant-suited, sweet-voiced, *lying bitch* that is President Vale.

I did swear I would kill her the next time I see her, didn't I? *This is just one more sweet reason to add to the list.*

"I'm still hungry," complains Andie, earning another grunt of annoyance from the giant, stoic Todd.

C sighs, then turns her face toward mine. "Food is running scarce in these lands. The woods out far to the east are dying off at an alarming rate, and our scouts have had to travel out farther and farther to gather fruit. The ugly truth is, life is quickly becoming less possible here." Her eyes flick to John's, then back to mine. "We need to get back to the land of the Living … if we have any hope of surviving in the long term."

There is a snap of a twig.

All of us draw silent.

Our eyes dart around, staring into the darkness that surrounds us.

Nothing moves.

Then I spot a tiny red light in the trees.

With a fizzling, sputtering noise, the light grows at once, revealing itself as a metal flare, and it illuminates the shape of a soldier dressed in full body tech armor, heavy and clunky, his face hidden behind a thick metal helmet.

Todd instinctively steps in front of C and Andie, an act of protection. John and I rise off the floor together, eyes wide with caution, prepared to run.

And then the soldier speaks, his voice deep and wary: "Jennifer Steel?"

My throat goes dry.

Who is this? How does he know my name?

Two more soldiers emerge from behind him, flanking the man on either side, both similarly armored from head to toe with their faces hidden behind helmets.

"Who—Who are you?" I manage to ask.

"I am a soldier enlisted by Skymark for the purpose of seeking you out and bringing you to our encampment. Are you Jennifer Steel?"

Encampment? Skymark? "Y-Yes, I am," I stammer.

"*Jen*," breathes John in warning.

"Come with us," commands the soldier.

I give John a look of concern, then glance back at the others, as if asking them without words whether I should go along with the soldiers.

C steps in front of Todd, her eyes sharp, suspicious, and full of malice. "Never trust a Skymark soldier. They only obey whomever pays them more. They are men and women without honor, as soulless as the Dead."

"We have food and provisions for your friends," states the soldier, ignoring C's statements. It's difficult to say where he's looking, covered by the metal, pointed shape of his helmet as he is, which makes his face look like a big steel beak. "This is an urgent issue that requires you to come with me, Ms. Steel. You will not be harmed."

"And if we resist?" I ask defiantly.

"I cannot force you to come with us," he answers. "But if you resist, you'll be left on your own out here in the wilderness, and I will have to report to Commander that you have refused to come. Then we will have to find another means to complete our dire mission."

"And what is this 'dire mission' exactly?"

Winter's Doom

"That cannot be disclosed here."

I glance down at his waist and his hands, then also at the others. *They aren't armed*, I note.

"Jen ..." murmurs John.

"We'll go with you," C announces. I glance over at her and the others, surprised. She gives me an assured nod. "We have your back."

If these soldiers came from Skymark, they might have an important message or mission that could change our situation here in the Sunless Reach. Why else would they be here? It has to be important.

Perhaps they've changed their cruel minds about our sentencing. Maybe depositing us here was just some kind of warning, and now they're ready to take us back home and set things right.

Or maybe all of that is some sick, weak, wishful thinking.

I take a deep breath. "I'll come see your Commander."

"Good." The soldier nods his helmeted head at each of us. "Follow me, then, and stay close."

With that, the three soldiers begin marching away, and after one more glance over my shoulder at C and her friends—and John with his dark, wary eyes—I follow the trio of soldiers into the twisted, shadowy woods.

It isn't long before the stark, cool-white light of metal fluorescents spills through the spindly trees. Before our eyes, we find sheets of metal that have been erected for walls. Through a small steel gate, the soldiers lead us, and as we pass through, we watch other soldiers standing atop the erected walls staring down upon us, their faceless helmets unwelcoming and cold.

I take hold of John's hand, gripping it with assurance.

He squeezes back as we walk along.

Within the metal walls rests a small encampment of tents. A portable furnace has been erected in front of one of them, around which soldiers—their helmets off—eat and talk amongst themselves. They go quiet as we pass, their eyes following us suspiciously.

We come to a stop before the largest tent in the center of the encampment. It's there that the soldiers stop my friends by lifting a hand. "Only Jennifer will be permitted in the Commander's tent, I'm afraid."

"No," John states. "We're going in with her. We—"

The soldier addresses me only. "Your friends can wait by the provisions tent where they will be fed, and any wounds tended to. Only you are allowed to meet with the Commander."

"It's okay," I assure John. "I'll be fine."

John looks at me severely, then inclines his mouth to my ear to whisper, *"These are the same folk who sentenced us and threw us away to die. Don't forget that."*

"I know." I glance over at C. "Keep on your guard, *C for cautious.*"

Winter's Doom

Appreciating my poke at her name, C smirks, then replies: "Oh, I'm *never* off my guard, *J for justice*."

I give her a nod, then face the soldier. "Take me to your Commander, then."

I let go of John's hand, then follow the soldiers into the Commander's tent.

The tent is large enough to fit a long metal table with space to move around it. Upon the table is a map spread out with small beeping devices set all around it. At the end of the long table stands a bald man in a military suit with his back to me, half-shadowed.

"Commander," announces the soldier. "Jennifer Steel has arrived."

"Good," states the man.

Then he turns, revealing himself.

My jaw drops through the floor.

It's Professor Praun.

"Leave us," Praun commands the soldiers, and at once they depart, leaving me alone in the tent with him, just the long table and a map standing between us.

I can't believe he's here. "P-Professor?"

"Time is of the essence," he states, slowly strolling around the table, "so I will be *to-the-point*. I am a General for the Humans, working in secret for the government as the acting liaison between the Living and the Dead."

"Acting liaison between …?"

"The Human government has known of the existence of the Dead. You, of course, are well aware of that."

"Of course I am," I snap, my emotions bursting forth like fire. "I'm here because of my awareness of it."

"And it may be that awareness that saves you." Praun stops halfway down the table, then taps a finger on the map. "I have received communication that the Dead are uprising. You need not confirm it; I already know. We have sensors and satellites that read the number and location of the Dead. Their numbers have multiplied by a factor of twelve over the last ten hours alone. That is why I am here with a small team of trusted associates to negotiate and reestablish peace with the Dead. We have had peace secured for many, many decades. It is only now—upon your return here—that the peace is unstable. If you help us regain that peace, I will offer you *and your friends* something you gravely want."

I have so many unanswered questions, I'm not sure my mind can fit another one. I come up to the table. "You put that rock back in my pocket."

Praun stares at me, his eyebrow-free forehead flat and his eyes like glass. He doesn't seem to appreciate my abrupt shift in topic.

"You wanted me to bring that rock here," I go on. "You told me to convey a message, but failed to mention what that message means and *who* this 'queen' is."

Winter's Doom

In a firm monotone, Praun says, "I have no idea what you're talking about."

My eyes narrow. "Yes, you do. Don't play with me."

His eyes turn dark and his jaw tightens. "I neither said any words, nor put any such stone in your pocket. You are clearly and most certainly mistaken, Ms. Steel."

It's then that, tight-lipped, he nods toward a device on the table, which blinks between us.

I cast my gaze down to it, then realize.

We're being recorded, or someone else is listening.

I frown, unsatisfied. "Fine. Perhaps I'm ... *clearly and totally mistaken*," I mutter with too much force for it to be natural, rolling my eyes at the device. Then I eye him. "But if, hypothetically, I wasn't, it'd certainly be helpful to know *why* I've been given such a message. And the rock."

"Perhaps you'll find the answers you seek by simply completing the task I am assigning you." Praun places his hands on the table and gives me a stern, cold look. "Can I count on you to carry out this mission, Ms. Steel?"

My eyes drop to his chest.

The acting liaison between the Living and the Dead ... I'm not sure where it comes from, but quite suddenly, I find myself filled with suspicion. How does Praun know so much about the Dead? Why did he give me the rock and send me here with a message for some queen, whether it's Corpsey's sister or not? What isn't Praun telling me?

I grab hold of his wrist from across the table at once.

His eyes flash and he pulls away indignantly, but I maintain the grip and squeeze my fingers upon his wrist.

And that's when I know.

He yanks his hand away again, and this time I let him go. "Ms. Steel!" he exclaims in protest, his tone hard.

"You're one of them."

He grows still.

My eyes are scanning him now in a whole new light, from his bald, eyebrow-free head to his toes. There was no pulse. There is no blood in his veins. There is nothing that pumps in his chest.

Praun is one of them.

He's been one of them this whole time.

"I suppose it ... isn't of any consequence whether you know or not," Praun says after some time—and clearly for the benefit of whomever is listening to this through the device. "It's how I'm able to be a bridge between Living and Dead. I am a Dead residing among you, to maintain the peace that is so necessary. Of course the government should station me at a university so close to the narrow sea that divides our land from yours—just close enough to keep an eye on the Blight to ensure it and its inhabitants stay exactly where they belong."

"And those inhabitants include people like me, John, and President Vale's own son now?" I ask acidly.

Winter's Doom

"Jennifer. None of these things matter. I told you that I am here for a very urgent, time-sensitive matter. The Dead are uprising, as you well know, and all of your lives are in danger. I am here to fix that, but ..." He clenches his teeth, rights his posture, then addresses me in a far calmer tone. "But I need your help."

"Why should I help you at all?" I challenge him. "For all I know, you're part of the reason I've been thrown here with my friends to die."

"If you perform the task I am about to give you ..." Praun's eyes meet mine, and the look in them is softened and sincere. "I am prepared with direct orders from the government to bring you and John back home safely."

I take a step back from the table, speechless.

"The charges would be dropped, your sentence and your crimes *forgiven*. The government will secure you a spot in the distant countryside to live in peace. The only condition is that your ban from the campus of Skymark will be upheld, and you will not be allowed there again."

At once, I feel the breeze of the countryside on my skin. I smell my mother's cooking in the morning. I feel the soft sheets of my bed over my body, cocooning me. It is a painfully seductive dream, the picture Praun paints.

"The choice is simple," he says coolly. "Complete my task and live in peace, or decline and stay here to die."

There is more at stake here than just my pride.

If what he's saying is true, John's fate also rests in my hands. *And maybe the lives of a few others, too.*

I take a breath, then look at Praun. "I'll do it if *all* of the Living here are taken home, too."

Praun's jaw tightens. "That isn't possible, Jennifer."

"Of course it's possible. You have the power. You are here to stop a Dead uprising, which is clearly an actual threat to the land of the Living, otherwise you wouldn't be here at all. So let's make it happen," I demand, feeling bold. "All of our lives ... or no deal."

Praun's left eye adopts a subtle twitch.

His fingers drum along the table with irritation.

"Fine," he at last relents. "All of the Living here ... will be included in the agreement. But ... the task must be completed to my *total* satisfaction."

"Deal." I cross my arms. "What's the task?"

"The task ..." Praun taps a green button on the device in front of him. It issues a short, low-toned beep. "... is a delivery."

I frown, confused. "A delivery ...?"

The opening to the tent swishes as a soldier escorts someone inside—a young man dressed in camouflage pants and a form-fitting olive green shirt, his golden blond sweep of hair peeking out from under his military cap.

My eyes grow double.

"Hi, Jennifer," says Connor Easton.

Chapter Eight

The Delivery

I stare at him, unable to manage even a "hi" in return.

Connor comes further into the tent, glances at Praun, then turns his watery blue eyes onto me. "I … I just want to say that I'm sorry. For testifying against you in Court. My parents … they told me I needed to do it. And the school. And President Vale. I … I'm sorry."

"I know," I say at once, and despite not quite knowing any of that until this very moment, all of it seems to click neatly in place. "I understand. Your brother, your parents. They expect a lot from you."

Connor swallows, then gives me a short nod. "And I forgive you. I … I *know* that if you could have, you would have let me off that hovercraft."

I try a tentative smile his way. "Thank you, East."

At the use of his nickname, Connor smiles back.

Praun, clearly at his limit of sentimental exchanges, clears his throat. "The peace offering is simply this. You will deliver a package to the leader of the Dead. I will send

Connor with you, as best suits a delivery boy to help with such a delivery."

With that, he takes hold of a small, smooth black box which had been sitting at the end of the table this whole time. It looks made of metal, wrapped in a single yellow string that crisscrosses over its top. He sets it on the table between us right on top of the map. The box is about two square feet in volume—an eyeball's estimate.

"The package must not be opened before it reaches the Dead," Praun explains, "as it contains something quite perishable if exposed to the harsh environment here for too long. It will be an offering of peace and a show of our gratitude for the continued harmony between Living and Dead. It is something they want."

I can't take my eyes off the smooth, sleek thing. Leave it to me to be suspicious of everything and everyone in this world, after what I've been through. "What is it?"

"It isn't of any Living concern," Praun states.

My eyebrows pull together. "Professor ... General ... Commander Praun, whatever the hell you're called ... I *respectfully* disagree," I say with little respect. "If I don't know what I'm delivering, then I will not deliver it."

"J-Jennifer, he said it isn't of our concern—" Connor tries to say.

But then quite suddenly Praun has a change of mind. "It's a delivery of prime blood."

Winter's Doom

I blink. "Prime ... blood?"

"Prime blood," Praun repeats more firmly. "And it is a large amount of it, despite the seemingly small size of this box. Enough to satisfy the tongues of every Dead on this very continent tenfold. Just a drop will give them the ever-coveted feeling of being *almost alive*. With just a drop, one can see the sunlight at last, see the real sky, feel unfiltered excitement, feel deep pleasure ... and otherwise experience what you Living do. I am well familiar with the feeling myself, despite not having tasted of blood in three and a half centuries." He gazes down at the box as if peering into the face of a lover. "How I'd so covet a drop right now, if I were allowed. Blood ... it is the greatest commodity to the Dead."

I frown. "So we're a blood bank now?"

My question stirs Praun from his bloody dreams. "This package shall be. And with the help of Connor, you will deliver it directly to the leader of the Dead. I will know if it has arrived, as we will track the package every step of the way. From our satellites, we have determined that the majority of the Dead are residing right now in the city from which you just escaped. After's Hold, I believe you call it. You will return here with Connor and your friends by tomorrow morning after this delivery, and we will depart in two government hovercrafts, which are suitable to carry well over one hundred souls each."

I doubt I'll be able to find thirty Living among us. Maybe not even ten. Still, something about this doesn't feel right. "Why not deliver it yourself?" I ask.

"They don't trust us, hence their uprising," answers Praun simply. "But they trust you. And you trust Connor. This package will regain their trust, I do expect. It must be the pair of you who deliver it."

I find myself wondering how old Praun is. *He hasn't tasted blood in three and a half centuries.* How long—and for how many generations of Living—has he been the so-named liaison between the Living and the Dead?

"Do we have an understanding of your mission?" he asks a touch less patiently.

I glance over at Connor. He merely stares back at me with a soft look in his eyes.

If there was something amiss, and Connor was in on it, he wouldn't be able to hide a guilty look from me, not in the way that the stoic, Undead, blank-faced Praun can. That much, I can guarantee.

So it is by that soft look on Connor's face that I turn my eyes back to Praun and state, "We will deliver it."

Praun nods once, satisfied.

Outside the tent, Connor and I cross the dusty, coldly-lit encampment toward the provisions tent, where I find John, C, and the others. John and Connor have a cool-mannered reunion, neither seeming comfortable enough to greet the other, and it is while refreshing myself with bread, meat, and a decanter of tea that Connor and I share with the others the mission we've been given.

"A delivery to the Dead?" John is beside himself. "Are we seriously expected to do this safely?"

"This isn't right," C says at once, her voice as sharp as a blade. "Delivering blood to a den of Undead lions."

"Better this blood than ours," grunts Todd, who still gnaws on a bit of meat, his jaw *clicking* with every chomp.

"We have to do it," I insist to them. "If we do, then we will be taken home. *All* of us. And that includes all the Living who are still trapped in the city. Dana. The strange pair who live across the street from you, C. The others who were dropped off here with us. Anyone who we ..."

My mind drifts to a certain someone I ran into the moment I arrived—a certain someone who was lost to the mists of the Whispers. *Where is Grim now ...?*

And my best friend Mari. Does she even count?

"Anyone who we ... can find," I finish, then swallow my bite of bread.

John inspects the box himself. "Looks like a standard metal pod ... the kind the government sends food and supplies in. Its freshness is ensured by staying sealed."

"Fairly standard," agrees Connor. "Maybe a bit nicer."

John grunts in response, squinting as he studies the box, running a hand over its surface.

Connor bristles, annoyed suddenly. "We should leave soon," he points out. "The Dead are convened at After's Hold, so we've been told, and the government is giving us until the morning to make the delivery and return here."

John squints at him. "Why in such a hurry, East?"

"Because the window of opportunity for peace with the Dead is closing, and ..." Connor swallows, then averts his eyes. "I ... I-I want to get back home. Soon." He eyes John, then me. "We all go home after this, remember?"

After a moment, John scoffs and shakes his head. "Are you really so naïve?"

Connor gawps at that. "What did you just call me?"

"You know too much now," John says, then points a finger at the Commander's tent, "and *they* don't take very kindly to people who know the truth about the Dead."

"They've been kind to me!"

"Of course they have—*so far*. You're the *poster boy* for obedience. But that won't last long."

"Oh, really? And what about all these soldiers here?" Connor argues back. "And the crew who rescued me from After's Hold, and you guys from that old rundown town? They all know the truth, too, and—"

"And they work for the government. You don't." John scoffs derisively. "You're just a lowly *delivery boy*."

"John ..." I breathe for a warning, tired of the two of them arguing.

Winter's Doom

"Not just a delivery boy for long!" Connor's face is turning red as he lifts his volume. "They said I'm going to be promoted within the company. I could even learn how to pilot a hovercraft someday! My own hovercraft!"

"You're a child," John spits back at him. "A gullible, foolish, naïve *child*."

"Guys." I come between them just as Connor makes a move toward John, dropping my bread to put a hand on either of their chests, keeping them apart. "Look, I know there's bad blood between some of us, but—"

"No. Just a big *box* of it," grunts John, fuming.

"We've been pitted against one another," I keep on, firmly, *"because* of the Living government. All of us have felt the injustice." I look at C, who regards me in a curious light, her eyes full of respect, drinking my words. "And it's time we put our personal feelings aside. This might be the answer, our mission. It might not be the answer. But no matter, us Living have to stick together now."

Connor, who looks like he's a second away from crying or spitting or screaming, forces himself to take one deep, long breath. It sounds more jagged and terrified than I think he intends, but it succeeds in its effort to calm him. "F-Fine," he finally manages to say.

John doesn't say anything at all. He just steps back, his face stern with emotion.

I guess this is where I leave well enough alone.

"As soon as I finish this stale, tasteless chunk of bread and swallow my equally tasteless tea," I then state to the pair of them, "we leave for After's Hold."

With that, the six of us settle in place, and I continue to finish my refreshments in a still and silent peace.

It's only a minute and a half later that our less-than-merry party of six depart the encampment. The black box is carried by Connor, who seems the most content when he's committed to the task he's been assigned. John and I walk ahead of the group, leading, while C, Andie, and Todd pick up the rear protectively, their eyes scanning the dark trees as we pass through them.

We are silent for a long time, no words exchanged between any of us. Only the noise of crunching twigs beneath our feet are heard.

I guess that's for the best.

We must be going a slightly different direction than before, for we never cross paths with the half-collapsed cabin. All we see in all directions is the dark forest and its countless, leafless, lifeless trees.

Twice along the way, Andie collapses, then whimpers to the others about being tired. After the third time the boy falls, Todd grunts irritably and slings the kid over his shoulder, opting to carry the president's son instead.

"I don't think we've slept in over twenty hours," John points out to me after some time.

"I can't feel my feet," I admit. "My eyes have a fuzzy sensation, like I'm sleeping with them open somehow. I worry if I stop, I'll fall asleep for three solid days."

"I would've expected to be back at the city by now."

"I guess walking all the way back takes a lot longer than when we were running for our lives."

John snorts, finding that funny. Then he puts an arm around my waist and plants a kiss on my lips. *"Keep strong, Jen. We'll be home soon."*

I find myself smiling at the fantasy of that … despite the doubt swelling in my heart. Has John had a change of heart regarding whether the government is to be trusted, or is he just saying that to boost our spirits?

After another long period of silent trudging through the woods, I peek over my shoulder at Connor. "Is that box heavy yet? Want to trade off with one of us?"

"I've got it," Connor insists.

I study him for a bit as we walk. "Are you excited about seeing Dana again? She's survived against all odds. I know it's only been a week, but that's a very long time here in the Sunless Reach."

"Yes, I'm happy to see her," he says, though his voice is lackluster and small. I can't tell if it's because he's tired, or perhaps his concern for her ended when he presumed he would never be back in this place, thinking her to be as good as dead.

Or maybe Delivery Boy East is just trying to be a super serious adult about all of this.

John steps in front of me at once, protectively.

I stop, followed by Connor, C, and Todd. Andie lifts his head off the giant's shoulder to peer at us with alarm. "W-Why'd we stop?" he asks in a tiny voice.

His question is answered as a figure emerges from the dark ahead of us.

I come around John at once when recognition dawns on me. "Erick," I say, for a moment forgetting the name I'd given him: Corpsey.

He stands there before me, his slim, awkward posture, with a strange and faraway expression. He doesn't seem to regard John or any of my companions, as if they might as well not exist. "Winter," he greets me, a note of humor in his soft, odd voice.

It's strange that, of all the creatures and people in this world—Living or otherwise—I don't seem to question my trust in this one. Ever since the first moment we met in that overturned hovercraft, I've felt a strange, comforting connection with him.

"What are you doing out here?" I ask, curious.

"My sister's impatient. I did warn you that she'd find you, didn't I?"

"You did," I agree, "and she stormed After's Hold with all her Dead. Some of them destroyed a greenhouse full of fruits and vegetables the Living needed to survive, by the way," I add sourly. "Be sure to thank her for that."

"I'm sorry," he murmurs instead.

John brings himself to my side, asserting his presence. It does little to intimidate Corpsey. "What do you want?"

Corpsey's eyes remain on mine when he answers. "I am just here for Jennifer. I am to collect her safely and bring her back to After's Hold, so that she may lead the Revolution, as is her whole purpose here."

"I appreciate that very much," I say, as if addressing a taxi driver. "But in lieu of a Revolution, I thought I might arrive with a gift instead. A gift for your sister."

Corpsey lifts an eyebrow. "Gift?"

His glassy eyes flick over to Connor, then drop to the box in the delivery boy's hands. He stares at it a good and long while, not a muscle in his body moving.

It's impressive, how still the Dead can become—as still as a photograph, or a shard of dull rock.

Much like the one I lost in the Whispers.

"It is something you want," I assure him, "and I think it is something that will appease your sister's thirst ... in more ways than one."

He purses his lips, staring at that box. "I'm intrigued."

"You won't need to be intrigued for much longer," puts in John tersely. "Lead us to After's Hold with this delivery. Then you'll never have to see us again."

Corpsey's eyes fall back onto me. "But I have grown rather fond of seeing you. I actually *like* the Living."

"Sure, tell that to your sister," retorts John bitingly.

"I have," he replies simply. "But she would rather see the world wrapped in *Undeath*. I have more of a mind to share it, I think. This is why it's of utmost importance that you take your position as leader of our Revolution, dear Winter. It may be you—"

"*Stop calling her that*," bites John.

"—who is the one to unite Living and Dead once and for all," he finishes anyway.

I shrug. "Maybe. Or …" I gesture toward Connor and the box in his arms. "Perhaps our gift will change your sister's mind entirely about her Revolution."

The tiniest trace of a smile touches Corpsey's thin, dry lips. "Alright. My curiosity is piqued to its max. Let's head off to After's Hold to meet with my sister with your gift and see for ourselves, shall we?"

With that, Corpsey turns and begins to lead the way. I give an assured nod at my companions behind me—C, Todd and his extra weight Andie, Connor and his box, and John at my side—then follow Corpsey.

The walk is long, but with Corpsey leading us, I feel strangely safer. What adversaries do we have here but the Dead themselves, and if we are accompanied willingly by one, what have we to fear?

Winter's Doom

Except maybe rabid, wild dogs.

Of course, that thought has me thinking once again of Grim. Maybe he got turned around in the Whispers and is simply holed up in that rundown town south of it. Or he might have made his way to After's Hold by now. Or he ran all the way back to the Necropolis and is hiding high atop that rice silo tower, combing the distance with his eyes for any sign of life.

Maybe he's dead.

Soon, the walls of After's Hold loom over us. We must be approaching from some different side, because I don't recognize this part of the wall. A door at its base is opened, and through it we're led inside. Instinctively, all six of us Living are now walking rather close to each other. John is nearly pressed to my side, as if at any moment he will jump in front of me and shield me from some unseen attack. Connor hugs the package like a pillow with C right on his heels, her eyes scanning every single thing we pass, wary. Todd marches behind with a shuddering, wide-eyed Andie clutched tightly to his chest.

All of the activity from before has settled, and the streets are eerily quiet, despite all the new faces of Dead that now watch from every window, courtyard, and curb of the street. Not a single one of them makes a sound, all their eyes trailing us as we pass, still as statues.

"You lost your stone," notes Corpsey.

The streets are so silent that when he speaks, his voice seems to fill the entire city. "I did. In the Whispers."

"I know."

I study the side of Corpsey's face, putting it together. "Did you see it through your green one?"

"Yes. I saw your distress, too, when the Whispers … began to do what they do." A look of discomfort creases his face. "I'd very much like never to return there."

"That makes two of us."

"I had to pass through that *evil plain* with my sister and the army dragging behind us, in pursuit of you. I thought I'd be coming to your rescue, but the mists were gone, and … so were you." He seems to find something amusing. "But something else wasn't."

I frown. "What wasn't?"

When I look ahead, however, I find we have already reached our destination: the door to the Mayor's building.

And at that door stands a certain pale-faced Living.

I stop short, my eyes flashing. "Grim …?"

Grim neither smiles nor moves. "Jennifer."

An ugly scowl creases John's face as he attempts to step in front of me, but I put a hand on his arm, stopping him. "Really, John, are you planning on starting a fight with *every* man in my life?"

John's scowl fades as he stares at me incredulously. "It's because of this poet that any of us are here."

Winter's Doom

"And it's because of him I'm still alive." I face Grim. "How'd you get here, Grim? What happened back in the Whispers? Where'd you go?"

After a timid glance at John, the poet brings his soft, strange eyes to mine. "I was found by the Dead, actually. And ..." He lets out a dry chuckle, then reveals a certain item from his pocket.

My necrocite.

Grim takes two steps toward me. I lift my hand, as if compelled by some invisible force, and he drops the dark, unnaturally heavy little rock onto my palm.

"See?" Grim chuckles. "Feels nice, doesn't it? Right back to its rightful owner."

I study the rock, turning it over in my hand, then lift my gaze to his, questions in my eyes.

"Erick found me using the connection between the rocks," Grim explains, "since he could see me through ... well, you know that part already."

"My sister still doesn't know of its existence," states Corpsey, though I'm not sure for whose benefit he says it.

"They kept me safe among their ranks," Grim goes on, "and ... well, after hearing about the way in which they envision our world ... I realize perhaps it isn't such a wrong thing for them to want you for their leader." Grim smiles suddenly. It sits oddly on his strange, angular face. "You were right, Jennifer. There is *good* inside the Dead.

The Beautiful Dead, you called them. The world needs to know of them. You … You are their queen."

My gaze falls back to the dark stone in my palm.

I feel a deep, unsettling discomfort with everything now, a discomfort I haven't felt since I lost this rock in the twisting fogs of the Whispers.

Maybe it was better off lost.

"If you two are done catching up," Corpsey says, his gaze flicking back and forth between us, "my sister awaits them, and they have brought her a gift."

At those words, Connor lifts his chin and adopts a brave look on his rosy, youthful face—betrayed only by the noticeable trembling of his arms underneath the box.

His visible fear does nothing to settle my nerves.

"Come," Grim urges us, beckoning us forth. "I'll take you to Megan."

The uttering of that name hits me. "Megan …?"

"Yes. Erick's sister, of course."

I part my lips, then turn to face Corpsey, who only stares blankly back at me. "Megan is your sister's name?" I ask him. "She never told me her name. You never said it."

Corpsey shrugs. "I was hoping it would come back to you naturally … when you remembered Winter."

Megan … That's the 'new' name on the *Diary of the Dead* books my dad left me. This couldn't possibly be the same Megan, could it? Surely "Megan" was a far more

Winter's Doom

common name during the time of the Beautiful Dead, and there could easily be dozens of Megans.

Regardless, the name leaves me staring down at my stone once again, feeling as if a piece of the bigger puzzle is still missing—a piece that urgently and ever so desperately needs to be found.

"Come," Grim says again, pushing open the door at his back. "Megan waits for you. She'll be so excited you've returned, Jennifer ... and with a *gift!*"

I glance back at the rest of my companions, unsure.

C speaks up. "Go on and give them their offering." She nods toward the street. "We'll go seek out the others in the city and get ready for the trip back to the camp."

I nod at her. "Thank you ... *C for courage.*"

She smirks at that. "We'll see about the courage part." Then she turns and departs with Todd and the boy he still carries, who watches me over his shoulder as they go.

I turn to Connor. "Let's get this over with, East."

Connor grips the box tighter, then gives me a nod.

I walk through the door, John on one side, Grim and Corpsey on the other, and Connor following behind. We walk down the familiar long hallway that leads to the Mayor's room where a heap of discarded furniture, trash, and books stand over us. Megan—one-eyed, bald, and skinnier than a skeleton—sits atop the hoard.

The Mayor, nor Truce, are nowhere to be found.

And in Megan's one eye, there is a look of great relief and triumph when she sees me. "Ah, finally, *finally* you are back." Her voice is high and clear as a crystal, ringing through the room. "I'm so, *so* happy to see you, Winter. In fact, I don't even mind that you ran away. *Again.*" She twitches with a note of annoyance. "Regardless, I *knew* you would come back. You always do. You needed some time to sort your thoughts … to find yourself in this land, to find the *Winter* in you, right? So have you found her?"

If by some far stretch of coincidence this *is* the same Megan as the one who wrote the stories, then I happen to know quite a lot about her, even if I once thought it was some wealthy professor's fictional imagining.

And perhaps that will help me convince her to accept this delivery and abandon her war.

I start to climb the pile.

First a foot on an overturned desk, then a foot atop a bundle of books I hope won't slip loose. I take another step and squish a foot into something crunchy, then another into something papery. I find purchase on a chair, then another desk, then a sideways filing cabinet.

And soon, I stand with her at the top.

"Megan," I greet her, almost out of breath.

"Winter," she greets me back, her voice soft, her one eye distant and curious, as if she literally sees the memory of Winter right before her—instead of me.

Winter's Doom

"Your brother ... has told me a lot," I begin. "I know that whoever you think I am ... *Winter* ... is a close friend of yours. Very close. Someone you considered a sister."

"Yes, you are," she agrees.

"And while I may not remember her, or you ... I hope someday that I can appreciate what a beautiful soul you are, and the relationship we had." Against all my instincts, I reach out and take her hand, which seems to surprise her. "I may not be the Winter you're looking for, but ... I hope we will be able to unify our interests."

Megan blinks her one eye. "What are you saying?"

After a quick glance down at Connor, I give Megan a smile. "I brought you a gift. It's from the other side of the sea ... the Living ... and it's something you want."

Megan squints skeptically. My hold on her hand seems to turn rigid, uncomfortable.

"From the ...?" She seems incapable of making sense of that. "What ... What would I possibly want from them other than their world?"

"Something all the Dead want. You may be surprised by their generosity." I glance down the tall heap of trash at Connor once more, then give him a nod.

He glances nervously at Corpsey, then peers up at the pair of us. "I'm a delivery boy. My name is East. I-I mean Connor. This package is for you."

"Package," murmurs Megan thoughtfully.

"It's blood." Connor's eyes go wide. He shoots me a stunned look. "W-Was I not supposed to say that? Was the gift supposed to be a surprise? I'm sorry."

I turn to Megan, who looks increasingly confused by the odd presentation. "Sorry. The Living government is offering you ... a gift of prime blood. It's a large amount. A big enough quantity to give all your kind a taste twelve times over, I've been told. It's ... an offering of peace."

"Peace." Megan begins to descend the pile of trash, her footing so careful, she never stumbles once on her way down to the delivery boy. "Blood, you say ...?"

Connor backs away the closer the sister comes until his back slams against the wall, his eyes wide with fear, sweat dressing his forehead.

Megan stops in front of him. Her eye zeroes in on the package, a skeptical squint.

Grim, standing nearby, glances up at me, then says to Megan, "I would trust Jennifer with my life. She wouldn't betray you. She has devoted her life to seeking the truth about your kind. She is here because of that devotion."

Still, Megan stares at that box in Connor's hands, not moving, not speaking, her one eye unblinking.

Her brother comes forward. "Megan?"

"Is ... Is that what they think of us?" she asks softly, a tinge of hurt in her voice. "Blood? That's all we ... could possibly want? Or crave ...? A box of ... of *blood* ...?"

Winter's Doom

That wasn't the reaction I was hoping for.

I speak to her from the top of the mound. "It's the gift of life, Megan, even if it's somewhat … temporary. We know what happens when you taste human blood. It's your greatest resource here in the Sunless Reach. With just a drop, this … this place isn't so *Sunless* anymore."

Despite my words, Megan continues to glare with malice at that small black box.

Her brother reaches gently toward Connor. "I'll take it," he murmurs kindly.

Connor puts up no fight when he releases the box to the brother's hands and steps away, clearly glad to be rid of it. Corpsey turns the box over a few times, studying it with mild curiosity.

He notices that his sister is watching him. He smiles her way. "We can accept this gift … and yet still continue to negotiate with the Living. They're here, Megan. They flew two metal birds here—the biggest birds I have seen yet—with a number of their soldiers and officials, and set up a camp in the deep east woods."

Megan crosses her bony arms. "Alright. So then let's have a look. Let's see this … this *blood* that our kind so dearly desires."

I watch from the top of the pile, curious.

Corpsey nods approvingly at his sister. "There we go. It isn't such a hardship to show a little appreciation now and then, is it?" He pulls on the string of the box, then lets the smooth metal lid of the container slide right off.

There is a small *click*.

His face contorts, perplexed. Megan's does, too. The pair of them say nothing.

I look at each of them, waiting. "What's wrong?"

"I see vials of blood, but …" Corpsey squints. "The shape of the container is odd. Is there more blood held deeper within it?" He lifts his gaze up to meet his sister's, squinting. "And do you hear that? It clicks."

"John, you're the engineer," mutters Connor from the doorway, his arms crossed, a distant, muted grimace of repulsion on his face. "Can you get it to open fully?"

John steps forward with a grunt to take a look.

The box clicks again.

John stops. All the blood rushes from his face.

"What's wrong?" I ask from up high, worried.

"It's a device that looks like a standard shipment pod," he answers, "but it isn't."

Megan frowns, confused. "So what is it, then?"

He looks up at me, then chokes his reply: "A bomb."

John's voice is so small, no one seems to hear him for a solid three seconds.

All the air vacates my lungs. "A-Are you sure?"

"It's an obsidian bomb. It's designed to …" He barely has enough breath to finish his sentence, terror taking hold of his throat, strangling his words. "... to p-pulverize anything within a mile radius. Every ... Everything will be obliterated. All of us." John stares up at me, glassy-eyed.

That empty, disconsolate look on his face is really freaking me out. "John ...?"

"They lied to us." It's eerie how calmly John speaks. "They gave us an explosive device. They want us all gone, Living *and* Dead. They—"

"Then why hasn't it exploded yet?" blurts out Megan.

"Who cares??" shouts Grim at the top of his lungs. "Run, all of you! Run!! Get out! Warn everyone!!"

And with that, Grim sprints out of the room, just the soft sound of his shoes scuffling down the hall touching our ears. Connor, aghast, his face pasty and sickened, backs away into the hall, then turns and runs off.

The box clicks again.

Corpsey drops it and steps back, terrified. The vials of blood rattle within the container.

"It'll be too late," John breathes, his eyes on the box as it sits there on the floor. All the life has fled from his eyes.

I'm not one to give in so easily. "MEGAN! ERICK! RUN!" I command both of them. "GO! ALERT ALL YOU CAN, BUT RUN WHILE YOU DO! GO, GO!"

Corpsey grabs his sister's hand and hurries off. Megan lingers only a second longer with her eye upon me, full of confusion and darkness, before the pair of them flee.

I scramble down the heap of broken furniture as fast as I can manage, my every footfall dislodging books and broken slabs of wood along the way. The second my feet touch the ground and I slap my hand into John's, he comes to, as if waking from a terrifying nightmare, and together we tear down the hall and into the streets.

Megan is ahead of us, shouting at anyone who can hear her. "GET OUT! GO! RUN, ALL OF YOU! OUT OF THE CITY! GO!"

But it is only mayhem on the streets in all directions. No one knows in which way to run. There is no knowing how far the bomb's demolishing hands will reach—or when. In every direction, there is screaming, scrambling, and bodies crashing into one another in their attempts to flee their unseen enemy.

"I can't believe it, I can't believe it, I can't—" John keeps muttering under his breath as we run.

"RUN FASTER!" I cry out, pushing my feet into the ground with every step, building speed. "GO!"

"We're dead." John is nearly whimpering as we turn a corner and race for the city gates. "We're d-dead."

The pavement soon becomes the shattered slabs of the Broken Road of Destiny—the so-named highway that leads out of the city. I don't let a single crack in the road trip me, my every step placed with eagle-eyed precision as we run alongside each other.

Winter's Doom

It's a moment before we reach the gates that I realize Megan's brother has stopped halfway down the street, staring back toward where we came.

I come to a stop, alarmed. "Corpsey??" I call out.

A look of overwhelming dread has flooded his face. He doesn't move, frozen to the spot.

"Erick!" I shout at him, using his real name. "What are you doing?? Why did you stop??"

He stirs from his daze and turns toward me, his eyes full of pain. "It's the Mayor. Damnation. She's still in the building where the bomb is. She doesn't know."

"There's no time!" I shout back. "The bomb—"

"And Mari is with her."

All the rest of my words stick in my throat.

Mari.

Then he breaks into a run, racing back into the city.

"Erick!" I scream at his back, turning to go after him.

Until John grips my arm. "Jen, we can't!"

"John!" I protest, pulling against him. *"Mari's in there!"*

"We have to run, Jen!! If we want to survive—!"

I spend one more second staring into the distance at the chaos of the city where Corpsey vanished. The world shrinks away in this second, and all I know is that my best friend Mari is in that city, and the only Dead I have ever trusted is racing back into it to save her.

Then there is a blast of light.

I shield my face and turn away.

The world rips out from underneath me.

Stone and glass and the howling screams of a planet ripple outward like bullets from ten thousand guns.

I feel blood spatter across my face.

My feet leave the earth and I'm airborne.

Everything moves so fast that I can't even hear my own screaming.

The world flips around me—up, down, up, down—until I land somewhere far away with a cracking noise that fills my ears—crunching bones and scraping flesh.

Are those my bones?

Is that my flesh?

I dare to open my eyes, and at once, they sting. Dust, ash, and droplets of blood rain silently over me, filling the air and the horizon where tall, daunting buildings used to be. Everything is slow and soft and far, far away.

Sound returns like a rushing ocean wave—but all I hear is ringing, a thick iron bell …

Ringing, ringing, ringing …

"John?" I call out through the silence, and even my voice is so many miles away, as if it isn't my own at all. "John??" I try again despite the muted air, but everything I see is floating volcanic ash and dust. The scent of burning paper and sulfur drift into my nostrils, causing me to recoil from it, sickened.

Winter's Doom

Am I still alive?

"Jennifer!"

I sit up too quickly at the sound of my name. My head hurts everywhere. The world spins around me so fast, I can't stop it and have to lie back down.

"Jennifer, are you alright??"

"J-John? Is that—?" I blink several times. My eyes still sting. I taste the sulfur now, the taste growing worse with every word I utter. "John …?" I cough.

Then the loud ringing fades.

John's face is before mine.

Seeing him sobers me at once. "John! What happened? Where's Erick?"

"I don't know. We're outside the city."

"Outside? Did … Did everyone make it out?"

"We're alive …" he breathes, tears in his eyes. "We—"

I sit up again and look around. I recognize nothing. The tops of every building are gone, as if plucked from the earth like weeds by an invisible giant. Ash fills the air, floating past my eyes. High above, even the impenetrable grey blanket of fog has had a hole torn in it, the golden-yellow morning sun furiously piercing through.

"Jen, we have to go. The Dead, they …"

When I climb to my feet, I realize I can't hear anyone screaming.

I don't hear much of anything at all.

Except a ghostly whirring of the wind past my ears.

And John—and whatever he's saying to me, which I can't even focus on, too shell-shocked from whatever just happened.

"M-Mari …" I breathe, my eyes on the city.

"Jen, we can't stay. The Dead—"

"I have to find Mari."

"Jennifer …"

Heedless of John's warnings, I hurry down the Broken Road, ignoring the pain in my legs every time I take a step, and the ache that throbs in my head, and the blood that runs down my arm from a cut I can't see.

"We can't stay!" he calls out behind me as he follows.

I hurry blindly down the ashen streets. I don't see the appendages and half-blown-up bodies of the Dead strewn everywhere—the corpses of reanimated corpses. I don't see the fallen towers, nor the hissing remains of buildings that not a minute ago stood tall and proud, nor the bits of bones my feet are crunching on the ground as I run.

I don't recognize a single street.

I don't know where I am.

"Jennifer …!" calls out John, far behind me now.

Then I notice the familiar, distinctive door to the Mayor's building, somehow miraculously intact, yet all around it has been reduced to rubble. Was the door flung here by the blast? Where is the Mayor's building?

Winter's Doom

I keep walking over the unidentified debris, fear and panic racing through my chest, my eyes frantically searching for anything recognizable.

Until I realize the chunks of stone debris at my feet are the remains of the very building I'm looking for.

When I hear her voice, I stop.

I stare ahead, ash gently blowing past my face.

At first, all I see before me is the grey and colorless rubble. Then I realize one of the shapes on the ground is Megan, crouched down. "I'll never ..." she is choking to herself, her voice trembling with rage. "I-I'll ... never ..."

I slowly draw closer.

Deep, dark dread holds me by the neck, its long, cold fingers squeezing.

Beneath Megan, I see the remaining shreds of a body.

It's remarkable I even recognize it as one, with so little of it left.

"I'll never ... never again ..." Megan's words become strangled with a deep and furious grief. "... t-trust another *Human* ..."

My eyes drop to the slivers and ashes beneath her: the remains of her brother Erick, where a single green stone now rests, glowing with an angry, crackling power.

Chapter Nine

The Living World

There is nothing I can say.

Nothing I can do.

The figurative bridge I thought we were building with our gift to the Dead was just destroyed in a blast of light.

And so was Megan's brother.

Erick ... Corpsey ...

Reduced to ash.

There is no sign of Mari anywhere. The Mayor, I can't even find a clue of where the remains of a body might be. Maybe all the Dead here at ground zero were thrown halfway across the city by the explosion. Or turned to dust on the spot. I couldn't even begin to guess.

I don't touch Megan. I say her name three times, and she doesn't respond. What could I possibly say, anyway?

I didn't know the Dead could die.

I continue across the debris, numb to the stinging in my cuts and wounds. Down the road, I find the remains of Winter's Retreat, recognizable only by the peculiar color of its brick walls, one of which still stands, though it looks as if a lazy breeze could knock it over.

I accidentally kick into a long shard of wood.

Oh. Actually that was an Undead leg.

I won't venture to guess who that belongs to, or how many stray appendages I've already walked over, thinking them to be other bits of building debris.

It's farther down the road that I find Connor sitting on a giant chunk of cement, his jaw slackened, his eyes wide and staring at his hands in disbelief, paralyzed to the spot. "I thought she'd survive ..." he mutters to himself, and it isn't clear whether he's saying the words to me, or to himself, or to no one at all. "I thought—She ... She had survived the whole week. I thought she'd ... she'd ..."

It isn't until I glance at the rubble by his feet that I even see her.

Dana.

She rests on her side among a twist of metal and fallen rock, with just her head turned and staring upward, eyes open and glassy, as if the explosion had merely woken her from a little nap she was in the middle of taking. Her silks are thrown about her, some of them torn, some of them covered by bricks and gravel, some painted in blood.

Her lifeless eyes stare up into the sky, as if pondering one of life's great questions.

I can't convey any emotion but shock, staring at her.

"Is this my fault …?" Connor asks—again, his question aimed at no one in particular. "Did I … Did I do this?"

"No," I try to say to him. "East, you didn't—"

"I thought she'd … she'd survive …" Connor goes back to saying, as if he didn't hear me, as if I'm not here. "She's supposed to survive … And I … I …"

I don't even realize John's been following me until I spot him across the hills of wreckage, his strong silhouette painted against the yellow-gold sky. "Jen," he calls out to me, his voice twisted with worry. "We've got to get out of here. The Dead will be after our blood, those of them who survived. They'll think—"

"No." I shake my head, and my gaze drops down to Dana. I feel my heart turning to stone the longer I gaze down at her. "We're not fleeing from them."

Connor glances up at me, as if just now noticing I'm here. His muttering stops.

"We're going to join them," I state.

John parts his lips, but says nothing.

Connor's voice is as tiny as a mouse's. "J-Join them?"

"The Living did this to us. To all of us." I point off into the distance. I don't even know if I'm pointing in the right direction. "Professor Praun lied to me. To you, Connor. The government wants us all gone, even the Living still here, even their own kind. The Dead … *They* are our family now. *They* are our kind."

Winter's Doom

John stares at me. He looks genuinely afraid of my words, his face blank and his mouth agape, breathless.

I don't have time to process what that look means.

I turn and head back to where I came from, walking with conviction over the destruction. I don't check to see if John or Connor are following me.

When I arrive at the ruins of the Mayor's building, I don't just find Megan, but Grim too, who stands next to her now as she stays crouched over her brother's ashes.

Grim turns first, spotting me. "Winter's come."

"Good," says Megan, rising.

Then she turns, and looks at me with her eyes.

Two eyes.

One of them glowing and green—her brother's stone.

I take a breath before I speak. "Megan, I know you're angry, and perhaps some of that anger is directed at me."

Megan says nothing. She merely stares at me as I talk to her, her Dead eye dull and glassy, her Green one fierce and pulsing, like a green heartbeat.

Grim swallows, his gaze shifting fretfully between us.

I keep going. "I don't know how to impress on you that we had nothing to do with this attack. I was lied to by my own kind. They ... They wanted to get rid of *all* of us. Living *and* Dead. But I—"

"I know."

I flinch at her sudden response. "Y-You do?"

"Yes. Your friend *Grim* here told me."

I look at him, wondering what he said.

"About the deception of your government," Megan goes on, answering my unasked question. "Their lies. The way they twisted *justice* to justify casting you here to our lands. And I'm glad they've done this."

I glance down at the remains of her brother, then back up at her, worried. "You're ... glad ...?"

"Yes." She steps forward and takes my hand, a mirror of what I did before giving her the bomb that took from her the only family she had. "Because now you see."

"See what?"

"Why we must end them."

I feel the iron-cold slam of a gavel in her words. I have a dark suspicion the Dead's idea of justice might be far, far worse than the Living's.

And I discover I'm not afraid of it in the least. "Yes," I agree, gripping her hand even firmer. "They have taken our friends. Destroyed our families. And yet here we still stand, more alive than we've ever been. Even you."

I hear the shuffling of feet behind me. I turn to find John and Connor standing a few paces away.

"President Vale and Professor Praun intended for us to die in this explosion, too," I say now for their benefit. "They want every trace of the Dead and its secret keepers obliterated."

John doesn't seem as easily convinced. "But if Praun himself is Dead, and the government knows, then why didn't the government form a plan to get rid of *all* of the Dead—Praun included?"

"I …" My mind goes blank. "I don't know."

"I do," says Megan.

All of us turn to her.

When she smirks, the light in her Green Eye seems to darken, as if from a passing shadow. "You were sent here to awaken the Dead. Awaken, we did. All ten thousand. Then, with us gathered in one place, they sent a bomb with you trusted Humans to put an end to us Unliving. They needed Praun to carry it out. No doubt they'll have some plan to end him when he returns home after he's ended us … except they failed." I watch the bones of her jaw grind with her anger. "And the Human camp still stands in the deep east woods. I bet they're celebrating our demise as we speak, the arrogant Living they are."

"You're suggesting we fight back?"

From the devastation all around us, I notice for the first time small figures standing around us at a distance— the surviving Dead who had gotten far enough from the blast to not have been destroyed beyond function.

I look out at them, astonished. Even after the bomb, I count dozens of us who still remain.

Us. Living *and* Dead.

"They have metal birds," says Megan, "and we have survivors. And without another great big bomb to rip us apart, the Humans at that camp stand defenseless and ripe for the taking."

At once, I'm with her. "We will steal their hovercrafts, fill them with our survivors, and fly back across the sea," I declare, my heart thumping with excitement. "That side of the world has never seen the like of the Undead. They will fall to their knees."

"If we even *leave* them their knees when I'm done," growls Megan.

Dana … Mari … Corpsey … Damnation … Truce … All of the lives we've lost today, even the ones whose names I don't know … "We're going to avenge our lost."

"Jennifer, wait."

I turn at the sound of John's voice, lifting an eyebrow.

He glances at each of us, then implores me with his deep, pained eyes. "Those people across the sea … Many of them protested for us, sympathized with us, believed in us. Countless of them have been silenced by that same corrupt government. Who are we, if we raid the land of the Living and destroy them in the same way we've been destroyed? Eye for an eye, and the whole world's blind. We can't hurt our sympathizers, too."

Megan comes forward, and her Green Eye shimmers against the pale yellow light of the sun. "Heart for a heart, and the whole world's Dead," she returns. "Who cares about a few eyes? I've gone with just one for longer than I can remember, and now I've two again."

John ignores her. "Jennifer, don't do this."

It's amazing, what the power of Living hatred can do.

The power of Dead anger.

The power of *vengeance*.

"We have to," I tell him, "or else we'll all die here."

"The Dead *cannot* die," John growls, losing his temper as he gives in to desperation. "They're all just … broken apart, dismembered, torn to pieces. Their kind can endure through all of time, no matter what."

"Endure?" says Megan. She points a finger down at the lifeless, unmoving scraps that remain of her brother. "You call that 'enduring' …?"

John ignores her. "The Dead will find a way back after this. But the Living? That is something truly fragile. That's something that *can* be ruined forever. Jen, you may be talking about the extinction of *Livingkind* if we go through with this and invade our homeland."

Megan smirks, suddenly having a change of heart. "You were brave in your convictions back then, too."

John stares at her, confused. "What?"

"Winter always had a *John* by her side." Megan lets out one dry, mocking chuckle. At John's look of surprise, she lifts her eyebrows. "What? You thought you weren't part of the great history of the Dead, too? I do remember John and the way he stood up for the Living … until, of course, he died and became one of us, too."

"No." John steps back. "You're lying."

"You were happiest when you were Dead." Megan glances over her shoulder at Grim. "And you too, *Grim*."

Now it's Grim's turn to flinch. "Me …?"

"You and Winter had the most *complicated* relationship of all. Friends. Enemies. Friends again. Almost lovers." She shakes her head, then gazes back at me and John. "All of us are here now, centuries and *lifetimes* later. A reunion of old, old friends." She faces me. "Does my Green Eye not remind you of the old Megan? The way I once was? Or does it rather remind you more of the dubious, clever *Grimsky* and the terror he delivered to the world with his green flames of rage?"

I look up at Grim, confused. Grim returns my look with an equally blank, uncomprehending one of his own.

"Never mind it," Megan says with a sigh. "All that matters is I'm equipped with my Green Eye again, and I am ready to face your world with its full power … once I get a grip on that power again. It *has* been a while."

"You … *will* find that power," promises Grim, having quickly shaken himself out of his own stupor. He puffs up his chest, proud. "And we'll fight by your side."

"No, I won't," snaps John. "I won't have any of this."

I frown at him. "John …"

"Let him disagree with us for now," Megan insists. "It's only in his nature. He can't be blamed for it any more than I can blame *you* for not remembering Winter. He'll see the truth soon enough. Grim." She turns to him. "Help me gather all the survivors. We will depart for the encampment in the deep east woods immediately."

Grim nods. "I'm on it." And off he goes.

Megan eyes me. "Be ready. It's time for Winter, now more than ever." A look of misty nostalgia sweeps over her face. "Oh, how I've missed you. You were there for me after my brother died as a Living. You're here for me now after my brother's died as an Undead."

"I didn't know the Dead could die," I admit, voicing my private thought from earlier.

Megan takes my hand once more, giving it a squeeze. "Our time has come, my friend." And with that, she takes off into the dusty ruins to help gather the others.

"Jennifer …" John speaks gravely to my back. "I have followed you all this way. I've believed in you, ever since I stepped foot on that hovercraft with you, but …"

I face him. "I know you don't agree with this, but it's our way *home*. It may be our only way now." I glance at Connor, whose bright blue eyes stare back, scared, under a tangled curtain of blond hair. "We can't survive here. You know it. I know it."

John doesn't say anything more, frustration and hurt blooming in his eyes.

"I should've known better," says Connor quietly. "I should've known better than to trust the government at all, but ... is this really the answer? To help the Dead?"

"We're helping ourselves," I remind him, "and we're doing this for the Living we've lost. Our government must be brought down if we have any hope of surviving. You're in this with us now, Connor. That bomb was just as much for you as it was for us."

That statement seems to stun Connor worse than the actual bomb did.

"Jen ..."

I look at John. "We're doing this. And we're not going to back down."

With that, I pull free from my pocket the dark lump of necrocite Grim returned to me, grip it firmly, and cross the crumbled wasteland that was once a proud city.

It's a hundred and twelve Dead that Megan amasses. One hundred and twelve Dead who can still walk and function. Thousands lie in the ruins of the city broken apart, separated helplessly from their bodies, heads, or limbs. Thousands buried beneath the wreckage, put to new graves, lost for now. Thousands more who were turned to dust from the blast, their parts and their souls lost to the wind, destroyed beyond recognition, gone.

Winter's Doom

Megan's brother with them.

Mayor Damnation, most likely.

Truce, whose many mysteries are now gone with her.

And Mari ... my sweet Mari whom I swore to protect.

C, Todd, and Andie are nowhere to be found. It's my best guess that the brave trio either fled the city and are hiding among the trees, or else they, too, perished.

We don't have time to find out which is their fate.

We only have time to determine our own.

The woods are far less eerie when traveling with a giant army of over one hundred Dead. Despite my worry of what John thinks of me, or the doubt in Connor's blue, cheerless eyes, I feel strangely invincible. Even the endless blanket of greyness above the trees isn't scary anymore.

"You're bleeding," notes Grim after some time as we journey through the east woods.

"It's dried," I say back. "Scrapes and cuts and nothing. I was lucky."

"Yes, you were. And many others were not." He sighs with dramatic flair. *"For the wounds that bleed worst are the ones we cannot see, and if—"*

"I'm not in the mood for your poetry," I say dryly.

"Oh, but it was my best yet! You know, if there's any doubt within you, you should disinvite it at once. You're doing the right thing here." Grim nods toward me. "That stone ... it gives you strength."

"She's strong enough without it," John growls from behind us both.

Grim offers a straight-lipped nod for a response, then looks away as we continue on.

And I peer down at my stone, my palm sweaty from the effort of gripping it so tightly. Its impossibly dark face stares back at me.

Is Megan able to watch me through this stone, now that she wears the Green Eye?

But when I look up at her, I see her marching along with her Dead, seemingly unaware of what I do with my rock, no flicker of an expression on her face.

Maybe it was just a Corpsey thing.

An Erick thing.

I look down at my stone again as we walk, and I can't help but find myself frustrated by a piece of the puzzle that won't sit in place. If Praun is the one who sent the bomb to eliminate us, why did he make absolutely sure I had this stone in my possession? Was it really just to help amass the Dead all in one spot, like Megan suggested? And if so, why did he bother giving me that cryptic message to pass on to the "queen of them all" if he was just planning to lay us to waste anyway?

Why does it feel like Praun's mission still isn't complete?

"There, the encampment!" calls Connor from behind, pointing.

Winter's Doom

Indeed, the metal walls come into view, far sooner than I think any of us expected. And toward its gates, a hundred Dead and a handful of Living fearlessly march.

"BACK!" cries the soldier at the top of the gate, his voice trembling with fear. "Back, I said! Get BACK!"

The Dead storm the metal gates, heedless.

With our sheer number, it is only a matter of seconds before the sad, temporary thing gives.

"REINFORCEMENTS!" the soldier shrieks out with a wave of his hands. "REINFORCE—!"

The man is knocked off his perch and falls right into the crowd of angry, scrambling Dead.

I think that might have been his final half-word.

I'm nearly thrown off my feet by the Dead who swarm around us, flooding into the camp. The air is filled with the screams and shouts of Living, punctured only twice by a few feeble shots from a gun or two, which are quickly silenced as the Dead stampede inward, trampling the Living.

"The hovercraft!" shouts Megan through the madness, finally adopting our word for it, her voice strong enough to pierce the noise. "Grab it! Steal it before it flies away with its wingless metal! Go, go!"

I grab ahold of John's hand, overwhelmed.

All I see in any direction are the scrambling bodies of the Dead and countless beady, blood-hungry eyes.

"Jen, stay close," breathes John in my ear, pressed to my side protectively.

But I wonder who's protecting whom.

The Commander's tent has already been toppled, and beyond it, I see a hovercraft. Its ramp is lowered, and to my surprise, Connor is already boarding it, trailed by a thicket of scurrying Dead.

"Aboard, aboard! Get aboard!" cries Megan, her words miraculously heard over the noise of growls and grunts and shouts of both Living and Dead combined.

Moving with the crowd of Dead, I turn my face to John. "Where's Praun?"

"There were two hovercrafts before. One of them is gone," John points out. "He must've left after giving us the package to deliver and took some soldiers with him."

My feet slap the heavy ramp as we chaotically careen up its steep floor. "But why didn't they *all* leave? If they were intending to blow us up, why are there soldiers still here? They should've all left when Praun did."

John's pensive silence is his answer as we board the craft. I peer over my shoulder, glancing back at the Dead boarding behind us, unsure.

Something doesn't feel right.

I find Connor at the command console, worrying over the buttons, switches, levers, knobs, and blinking screens. "Can you fly it?" I ask him at once.

Winter's Doom

"I don't know," Connor admits. "This is confusing."

"John, we figured it out the first time, didn't we? We had no idea what we were doing, and we managed to fly one of these all the way across the ocean."

"Yeah, but ..." John inspects the board with squinted eyes. "The first hovercraft was a small one made just for deliveries. This is a military-grade government craft for transporting troops, officials, and war supplies. It's huge and far more advanced."

"We'll figure it out," Connor decides at once, quickly putting on that brave face of his—which looks just as terrified as it does brave. "Y-You can go check with the others. Make sure everyone's aboard. I'm ..." His bravery is gone at once. He turns his bright blue eyes at me. "I-I'm scared. Are we doing the right thing? Is this a mistake?"

I put a reassuring hand on his shoulder. "Once we see the shrinking look in the eyes of every government official we face with our army of Dead, and they realize the error of their ways, we'll know we made the right choice."

"Are you sure?"

I stare at his face a good long while. "Yes," I answer.

I suspect the long delay in my response is the reason Connor stares at me with worry in his eyes.

"Lift the ramp," I tell him. "Everyone is aboard."

The ramp is soon lifted, and after a short and trivial argument between Connor and John about which way to flip some of the switches and levers, a loud hum of energy ripples through the vehicle, and out the window, I watch the world descend.

When it's just ocean through the glass, John moves away from the console, his task complete, and throws his weight against a nearby wall, glowering, arms crossed.

I approach him. "John …?"

"I got us off the ground. I got us aimed homeward." He lifts his eyes to mine, dark and angry. "Don't ask any more of me."

His tone of voice hurts me somehow. "John. Don't forget what they did to you, too. Our government—"

"Don't ask any more of me," he repeats, then pushes himself off the wall and walks away, disappearing into a side chamber.

I grit my teeth and stand there at the front, watching the ocean pass under our feet. Connor, still near my side, glances over at me, uncertain, then decides to say nothing and returns to staring blankly ahead at the ocean.

I feel truly alone at a time when I need support from anyone around me I can trust. *And that number dwindles.*

I'm left to listen to the noises of the Dead.

Some of the Dead grunt like cavemen.

Some of them speak civilly and use words, and I hear: "After all this time …" and "Have you ever seen water so clear?" and "We'll finally be able to exist without pain!"

Winter's Doom

Some of them are silent as statues, staring ahead, their beady, colorless eyes as dry and inert as marble.

And I keep telling myself: *You're doing the right thing. You're going to make the government see the Dead for who they are. Maybe the whole world will realize they deserve to exist as much as we think we do.*

"This hovercraft is fast," notes Grim as he strolls up to my side, then leans against the console—earning him an annoyed glance from the stressed, hyper-focused Connor. "It won't be much longer before we're home, I suspect. Are you ready to face your fate, Jennifer?"

I turn to him and tuck a curtain of my white hair behind an ear. "Face my fate …?"

"To be their queen." Grim smiles my way. "You're so strong. I … I knew you were strong when we were just students at Skymark together, but … I underestimated just how strong you really are."

"I may be leading them now, but …" I peer at Megan, who is doling out iron weapons she found in a couple of crates in the back of the craft—long knives, swords, and clubs. "I think that role of *'queen'* is already well-fulfilled by the one with the green stone lodged in her eye socket."

"The Green Eye opens when the Yellow …" mutters Grim thoughtfully. "I wonder—"

"Don't say the words," I cut him off.

Connor glances over at us, overhearing, confused.

Grim, oblivious, frowns. "Why not?"

I smile apologetically at Connor, then pull Grim aside and lower my voice. "Praun said them to me, and he's proven himself an evil, murderous traitor, that's why not. I don't want those words uttered again. The only one of the Dead who knew those words was Erick, and he's …" I sigh and look away. "Well, he's gone, and I'd like those words to die with him. If Megan hears them, there's no telling how her mad mind will interpret them."

"Hmm …" Grim nods slowly, then gazes out at the endless ocean. "Perhaps you're right."

I sigh and shake my head. "I wish sometimes I was never involved with the Dead … or pursued studies of them, or ever learned the truth."

"You ever wish you could start over?"

"Yes," I admit without thought. "Maybe I could've lived my life in peace, and some other poor girl born with winter white hair can take on this foolish burden."

"Winter white …" Grim takes my hand. "You're not alone in this, Jennifer. You have many people who care about you, and many people who—"

I pull my hand from his, uncomfortable.

He swallows, then retracts his own hand. "Sorry."

"It's fine."

"I was going to say … You have many people who …" He sighs. "… who would do *anything* for you." I feel Grim staring at the side of my face. "You have so much power in you ... and so much power in that stone."

"So you keep saying." I look at him. It isn't the first time I've turned to Grim with suspicion in my eyes. "What aren't you telling me, *Gill McAlister?* What do you know about this piece of necrocite that I don't?"

Grim stares back at me, lips parted, breath held.

And then through the air cuts a voice: "LAND! I SEE LAND!"

At once, the one hundred and twelve Dead rush up to every window and glass wall. Indeed, across the ocean, the faintest hint of land is now visible, and with every second, with every heartbeat, with every breath, the land quickly draws closer and closer.

As does the vast, tall, spectacular skyline of Skymark University, shimmering in the golden-yellow sunlight.

I don't think I've ever seen the whole campus from this angle. It looks as beautiful as it does dangerous, its tallest buildings appearing like sharp glass knives stabbing the fragile sky, shimmering with the fiery, golden-yellow gleam of the sun.

"Whoa," breathes Connor in my other ear, similarly taken by the view as I am.

I peer across the command console at John, who has come up from wherever he had gone off to, and even he appears awed by the sight, his warm eyes unblinking.

The sight of him hurts me now. I wish I felt alright with him. I wish we were all on the same page here and I didn't feel like I was doing something wrong.

I wish I didn't feel so alone in this conquest for justice I've brought a whole army of Dead with me to pursue.

"Winter."

I turn around. Megan stands before me, and at her back, the Dead have gathered, all their eyes on me—*well, those of them who aren't still glued awestruck to the windows.*

"Megan," I greet her confidently, shrugging off—or perhaps casually accepting—her use of the *Winter* name.

"You know the lay of the land, since this place is your territory." She nods toward me dutifully. "You will bring us to the leader of the Living."

The leader of the Living? "I ..." *Goodness, where do I even begin?* "There isn't exactly a 'leader' of the Living. That is Skymark University, which is where John, Grim, and I are all from. The, um ... 'leader' of Skymark ... is a cruel, sweet-faced woman named President Vale, but—"

"Is she like a Mayor?"

I shrug. "Sure."

"Then you will take us to this President Vale," Megan decides. "We will first conquer the City Of Skymark, then take on the rest of the Living World tomorrow."

I'm not sure Megan understands what a university is.

I'm not sure it matters.

Winter's Doom

"Where do I land?" comes Connor's voice suddenly. "We're almost there. But I need to stop the hovercraft somewhere. Where do I—?"

"In the grasslands outside the campus," I answer. "We will get into formation there, then march upon them from the south side. It will be the quickest path to the administration building where the President and those in charge reside. They won't see us coming."

Megan studies me. The look on her face is made all the more eerie by her new Green Eye. "This *President Vale* will be *mine*."

I smirk, for once feeling like Megan's taken the words right out of my mouth. "Trust me. That woman has been on my *to-kill* list for quite some time, too."

Megan lifts her iron sword and faces her army. "My Beautiful Dead, it's nearly time to Rise!"

A unified cheer of grunts and shouts and, *"For Winter!"* blast back at us, full of strength and drive.

I flinch, startled again by the unified vigor of Megan's terrifying Unliving army.

And again, a small voice inside me says: *You're doing the right thing.*

The hovercraft lowers upon the grass some distance from the university, and quickly, the hum of its engines fade. Connor steps back from the console, eyes wide, as if astounded with himself that he was capable of such a task.

The Dead begin to group around the ramp, waiting for it to be lowered, all of them brandishing their weapons with a hungry gleam in their eyes.

When the ramp lowers, the Dead steadily march out of the hovercraft. As they go, I lift my eyes to find John's across the console from me. For a moment, we simply stare at one another.

Then he pushes away and heads toward the crates of weapons, fishing around in its contents for something suitable for himself. Connor, after a moment's reluctance, approaches the crate to do the same.

I come up last, squint into the crate, then pull out an iron sword. The blade end drops quickly to the floor with a loud *clang*. "Oh … these are heavier than I expected."

John abandons his own pursuit of a weapon and takes the sword from my hand. I watch him, my eyes desperate for some kind of support or compassion from him. All I get is a stony expression on his face as he studies the iron sword, feeling the weight of it.

"It's a broadsword," he finally says, his voice gruff and deep. "Heavy … Medieval … These weapons are from another time."

"The Dead are from another time," I joke.

John stares at the flat of the blade, brooding.

Connor pulls out a pair of long knives, then sighs. "None of these weapons are a match against guns. The security officers at the university will likely have guns. I'd bet the government left authorities of their own on the campus, just to ensure peace." He looks at me. "What's the point of having weapons of our own?"

"We're far more vulnerable." I press the handles of the pair of knives he selected toward his chest. "Better to have some kind of weapon than none at all." My eyes catch sight of another weapon, which I quickly grab from the crate: a smaller sword that, to my surprise, balances perfectly in my grip. "Now *this* one, I can use."

"No steel weapons at all …" John frowns, frustrated by something on his mind.

Connor and I look at him. "What is it?" I ask.

"All of this is too … convenient." John runs his hand gently along the flat of the blade, pensive. "Praun puts us into a state of war. Praun also knows I'm an engineer and would have recognized the obsidian bomb. Praun leaves us a hovercraft. Praun fills its armory with iron weapons, no steel." He faces me. "Doesn't all of this ring as rather strange to you?"

"Of course it does," I answer him, frustrated. "As does a lot of things lately. I don't know whose side Praun is on. I don't know if we're walking into a trap, or if we might actually succeed in changing the minds of the Living government. I don't know if I'm about to put President Vale's head on a spike." I narrow my eyes. "But whenever

I think about Mari's cheery face, the glowing makeup on her round, rosy cheeks, and the last time she hugged me as a human being ... I want to destroy things. Whenever I picture President Vale's perfect fall of ruby red hair and her pristine ... stupid ... pantsuit, all white and spotless and *evil* ..." I clench my teeth, then shake my head. "I just want to take deep pleasure in watching everything she's built up over the years burn to the ground."

John's eyes grow double at my words. "Jen ..."

"They've destroyed our lives. Whatever we were, it's gone now." I grip my weapon tighter. "I don't care if Praun had a part in this, whether to help us or hurt us. For all we know, it was the government who sent us the bomb, and Praun was entirely unaware. Or it could have been President Vale herself who ordered the bomb. No matter how you paint the picture, there's blood on all of their hands."

John puts down his sword and takes my free hand into his. "Jen, I will stand behind you. I will support you. But only if you tell me that you understand the full severity of what we're about to do. There is no turning back after we walk down that ramp here in the Living world and lead the Dead to Skymark."

I swear I can feel his heartbeat in the strong grip of his hand. His warmth. His fervor. His devotion.

I lean toward him and put my lips to his.

Winter's Doom

John sighs against our kiss, gripping my hand tighter.

When I pull away, the soft look in his eyes reminds me of the first day we met, rushing out of the rain and into my condominium, and I felt his heart racing through his wet shirt.

"I think I already made my decision the day we met," I tell him quietly. "We were never destined to live normal lives. We were destined to *change* the Living world."

A pinch of fear enters John's eyes.

I'm not sure those were the words he wanted to hear.

"Guys," comes Connor's voice—who's been standing there staring at us awkwardly the whole time. "The Dead are waiting for us. Down the ramp. They sound restless."

I let go of John's hand, then give a nod at Connor. "So let's go meet them."

Chapter Ten

Closing The Yellow Eye

Megan and the Dead are forming lines and organizing. Next to her, I see Grim, who stands as proudly as the Dead—and whose pale, chalky complexion and ghoulish eyes nearly blends him in with the rest of them.

As I approach, the Dead respectfully step aside, creating an aisle from me to Megan. I nod at them as I walk through them, then join my alleged best friend and once-sister at the front.

"If they spot us approaching with weapons drawn," I warn her, "they may have orders to attack. I don't know what awaits us."

"We'll be ready no matter," states Megan boldly.

"Good. Then let's move."

With that, I march on. Behind me, a hundred feet move in unison, marching with me.

I've never felt such power in simple footsteps.

As the campus looms closer, I peer over a shoulder and find John walking alongside the Dead, his steely gaze forward and focused. Farther behind, I spot Connor, his hands balled into fists, and his eyes flitting all over the place, scared, as if expecting something to jump out of the grass at him at any moment.

The poor delivery boy looks more terrified now than he did in the Sunless Reach.

That's when my gaze moves past him toward the hovercraft we've left behind, and I notice a long, dark trail where the Dead have marched. I don't quite make sense of it at first, wondering if it's mud we've tracked from the Sunless Reach, or a very long, off-putting shadow.

Until I return my eyes to beneath our own feet.

And find that with every step, the grass beneath the Dead army curls away at once, withering, dying.

We're leaving a trail of *death* in the bright green grass where we march.

My eyes shoot forward, alarmed.

Is this really what I want? Is this the right thing?

"Class is in session," notes Grim from Megan's side with a pinch of amusement. He eyes me. "I see students."

I see them, too. We're approaching the south side of the campus where a few math buildings are surrounded by green, flowery courtyards. Along the stone pathways that cut through the flowers, there are students calmly walking to their next class, smiling and laughing with each other, books clutched in their arms.

It only takes one of them to spot us before everything changes. First, it's one student screaming and running away. Then another, then another, and soon, it's a chorus of shouting and scrambling as the students scatter over a discordant soundtrack of screams and the thudding of dropped books and backpacks.

"They're afraid," says Grim, a growing hunger in his eyes. "They're *smart* to be afraid."

I grip my sword tighter.

When we breach the campus grounds, we do not stop as we trample over the flowers and the grass on our way past the math buildings. The gorgeous flora turns grey and withered as the Dead at my back march forward. Like a disease spreading its dark, wormy fingers, the army of the Dead spread across the campus, fanning out on either side of me. Students continue to scream and race for the nearest building they can.

And there I walk on, as brave as I possibly can be, chin lifted and sword brandished.

I watch as students rush to the windows, staring in horror at us. I watch professors in those buildings quickly asserting control, despite looking just as terrified as the students they're ushering away to safer places. I watch even the underpaid campus security guards shrinking into nearby buildings, aghast. Not even they will stand up to the intimidating army at my back.

I smirk with dark satisfaction.

When we arrive at the foot of the long stairs that lead to the administration building, I find President Rosella Vale awaiting us at the top of them just outside the front doors, as if she has been long expecting us. A gentle wind blows past her face, tossing her red hair and making ripples in the silk material of her spotless white pantsuit.

"Jennifer," she calls down from the top of the stairs. "This is folly, to create such a disruptive demonstration with your … friends," she decides to call them. "I order you and your friends to stand down, to drop all of your weapons, and to surrender yourself before we are forced to take violent action against you."

Megan shifts with agitation next to me, gritting her teeth. Grim stands next to her silently, his eyes sharp and focused. All the Dead at our backs stand wielding their weapons and waiting with perfect stillness for an order.

I lift my chin and address the President. "You brought this on yourself with your false promises and lies! You—"

"If you do not surrender," the President cuts me off, her voice far away yet booming down the long length of stairs, "my authorities will be forced to open fire on you and all your friends."

It's then that I notice all the faces in the windows of the administration building. Soldiers armed with guns. I glance at other nearby buildings and find more soldiers with guns aimed at us. Dozens upon dozens of them with countless bullets of ammunition, no doubt.

A chill of dread settles in me.

We're outnumbered by far.

"Surrender now, Ms. Steel," calls out the President. "Tell your friends to put down their weapons, and I will allow you up to my office to discuss terms for your and your friends' surrender."

Megan burns her eyes into the side of my face. "Well, Winter?" she mutters quietly. "Is this the President Vale woman I'm going to delight so much in killing?"

I turn to her. Grim's worried eyes are on me, too. "Yes, this is her," I confirm, "but ... we may have a more pressing matter on our hands. See all of those people in the windows?" I point them out. "They have guns. Do you know what a gun is? It can stab holes in us from very far distances. They're like ... tiny metal arrows that can travel very, very, *very* fast."

Megan's face wrinkles up, and she casts her Green Eye and her Dead one all around her. She sees all of the faces. She sees all of the weaponry.

"We're outnumbered," I tell her, pointing out the obvious. "We cannot fight them. Not like this."

"You can't. But we can," says Megan coldly.

I look at her, alarmed.

Megan ascends three steps. "I will make *you* an offer,

Winter's Doom

Living President Vale of the City Of Skymark," she declares.

And with a flash of her Green Eye, the Dead army at her back shift like a machine, resituating, and at once, I find half of them armed with glass bottles of some clear, unknown liquid, and the other half lifting torches in the air, prepared and waiting for the call.

I can neither answer where any of those items came from, nor where they were hidden in the first place.

"Put down your *tiny metal arrows,*" states Megan with cold and fatal promise, "and you won't have to watch your precious city burn to the ground at the hands of the vengeful Dead."

I hear stirring at the windows. Some of the soldiers have fled their posts, abandoning their guns. Others stand strong, keeping their guns aimed right at us. Many more windows reveal students and professors watching this whole scene with disbelief and terror in their eyes.

I find their faces the worst to observe. My peers. My fellow students. My professors. Is Megan threatening to burn them alive, too, or is this all a bluff?

The President shuffles her feet uncomfortably at the top of the stairs. She glances to the left, then the right, her red hair set ablaze by the sunlight over her.

She doesn't know what to do.

I turn to Megan. "Let me speak with her before you do anything."

Megan keeps her deathful stare upon the President as she responds, "You have exactly one minute to negotiate with the Living before I set loose my flames."

Fear bubbles up in my chest. My head is spinning. "Megan, this isn't how we negotiate terms for peace. We can't do it with threats of fire and vengeance."

Megan allows exactly three seconds for my words to enter one of her ears and fall out of the other. "We tried peace," she states, bitterly biting each of her words. "My brother is gone because of that so-called 'peace'. We are beyond … *negotiations*. What I want is that President on her knees, begging mercy for her life. It is only then that I will decide whether to give it."

My insides are shaking. "Megan, please. I want to help you. I am angry, too. But we cannot destroy their world or else there will be nothing left for any of us to live in. Megan, listen to reason."

"I have listened to reason for a thousand years," she returns in an eerily calm, quiet voice. "Now, I will listen to my heart. Do you hear it?" Her eyes still trained on the President, she places a hand to her own chest, then taps it in rhythm with a heart I know does not beat within her. "The heart of vengeance. Of my brother. Of my lowly existence. The heart of my thirst for *blood*. And it beats, Winter. It is more alive than it ever was when I was a Living." The smile that spreads over Megan's face is full of lustful malice. "I used to fight for the Living when I held air in these lungs. It was so tiresome. And now I wonder why I ever tried."

"Because it's worth fighting for," I tell her, growing desperate. "Because if we start a war today, we risk losing everything."

"You're mistaken. The war started long, long ago." She peels her eyes from the President and turns them on me. The green one is darker than usual, churning with unknowable power. "Today, we *end* the war."

From high atop the steps, the President's voice comes in a cascading boom. "Jennifer Steel. This is folly and you know it. Soon, there will be armies on your heels. One hundred thousand soldiers. They will arrive flying over your heads and storming you on foot. You cannot win this battle. Your best and only option is to surrender right now—if your life and the lives of your friends mean anything to you."

It's only now that I realize by "friends", President Vale has only been referring to John, Grim, and Connor.

She doesn't regard the Dead at all.

Their fate is sealed, in her eyes. They will be ended today, the last of them that remain. Their threat will no longer be one for which a narrow ocean must divide us. President Vale has held us in checkmate this whole time, simply waiting for me to acknowledge it.

I know what surrendering to President Vale means. I am as good as dead. So is John. So are Grim and Connor.

Perhaps it was always our fate to be one among the Dead.

"You left me no choice, Ms. Steel," booms President Vale. "We open fire in ten … nine … eight …"

I face Megan, wide-eyed. "We can't—"

"Seven … six … five …"

"Jen!" calls out John from the thick of the Dead army, Connor at his side, terrified.

"Four …"

President Vale isn't allowed the chance to count the last three seconds. Megan's Green Eye glows furious as an exploding star, and with one unified movement of the hundred and twelve Dead, the sky fills with glass bottles thrown and shimmering torches flung like daggers.

Fire erupts at the base of every surrounding building. Fire erupts in every window that once held a brave soldier with a gun. Fire chases its way greedily up the steps of the administration building, causing the President to retreat at once through her doors.

I fall back into the crowd of the Dead as another wave of flame is thrown airborne. The bottles are ignited by the torches, and when they land, it's like a hundred bombs of liquid fire surging forth to feed upon the bricks, shatter the glass of every window, and swallow the classrooms from the inside out.

Winter's Doom

The Dead scatter, charging through every nearby door with manic excitement, weapons raised.

I spin around in bewilderment, overwhelmed, blinded by flames and screams and shattered glass.

A man flings himself out a window, screaming as he somersault through the air. I don't know if he's Living or Dead; I can't even tell.

People gather on rooftops, only to be confronted by grunting and growling Dead, who chase them to the edge, then laugh and raise their weapons as students, professors, and unarmed soldiers plummet to their deaths.

I slap a hand to my mouth, tears in my eyes.

What have I done?

John appears at my side, soon followed by Connor. Together, we race up the steps of the administration building where Megan and Grim have taken off running in pursuit of the President. The multiple fires at our back have grown triple already, their hungry tongues climbing up the sides of every wall, door, and window. I hear the crackling groan of wood and metal, structures threatening to collapse with the Living still trapped inside.

"We have got to stop her!" cries John as we race up the steps, our heavy swords wielded.

"Megan or the President??" I shout back.

The glass doors to the building are shattered, and it's through that jagged mouth that we plunge. Ahead, we spot Megan charging up the familiar winding steps where the President has fled. We race up the stairs in pursuit.

It's at the torn-open doors of the President's office that we come to a stop. The women are facing off, Megan's sword lifted and pointed at the President's neck. Rosella Vale has her hands lifted in surrender, her body trembling with such fear, I can literally see her red waves of hair as they shiver and shudder.

I step quietly into the room, afraid to startle anyone and cause a certain sword to jump. Through the floor-to-ceiling glass windows that stretch from one side of the room to the other, the fire and chaos of the campus blends into the yellow, fiery sky so seamlessly, one might think Skymark University floats in an ocean of lava.

"Jennifer," comes Rosella's voice, impressively even and calm. "Tell your friend to lower her sword."

Grim stands next to Megan, and his eyes find mine. He looks strangely excited, as if the thrill of Megan's vengeance has somehow become his own.

"If you burn our world to the ground," Rosella goes on, "then what will you have left to *live* in? You are still alive, Ms. Steel. This is *your* world they are stealing. Tell your friend to lower her sword, *now*."

The tip of Megan's blade, as if provoked by a child's dare, gently presses forward, kissing the President's neck.

Rosella shuts her eyes and swallows, trembling.

"Answer one question truthfully," states Megan, "and I will drop my sword."

President Vale doesn't move a muscle nor open her tightly-clenched eyes. She merely stands there, hands still lifted, shaking in her fancy, high-dollar boots.

"Megan ..." I try, speaking calmly.

Grim studies me curiously.

I come a bit closer. "Megan, please. We can resolve this another way."

"All she has to do is answer a question," Megan nearly sings, her voice so playful, I might suspect she enjoys her power over the President in this moment.

"But ... perhaps she can better answer it with your sword lowered ...?" I gently suggest.

"Yes," Rosella is quick to agree, her eyes clenched so tightly, she might be able to taste her own eyelashes. "Quite smart, Jennifer. Yes, I will answer your question truthfully, whatever it is ... if you lower your sword."

Megan shakes her head. "But the tip of my sword at your neck begets the very question I wish to ask. It would not make sense to lower my weapon."

Grim smacks his lips, fidgets, and drinks in the sight of every frightened reaction on President Rosella Vale's face.

I frown at him. He's enjoying this too much.

"So ask your question, Dead girl," hisses Rosella with just an ounce of breath in her tightened lungs.

Megan smirks. "The question is merely this: Are you excited to learn what comes next?"

The question makes the President's pretty eyes flick open. She stares at her in bewilderment. "Next …?"

"Yes." Megan tilts her head. "After I behead you. Are you curious what comes after Life?"

The President's eyes go wide.

For one half of a second, Rosella turns to flee.

The other half of that same second, Megan's sword flashes through the air like lightning.

The President's head drops to the floor with one soft, soundless spray of blood. Her body drops clumsily to its knees, seems to teeter for one and a half seconds, oddly balanced, before falling over with a nearly silent *thump*.

I drop my sword and slap both hands onto my mouth to swallow a shriek.

"Death … is the next evolution of Life." The calm, ponderous words come from Megan as she slowly circles the headless corpse of the President. "It is where *all* Life is headed, its final destination, whether you're a bird, or a tree … or a human being. It is the only thing in all of existence that is inevitable. *It* … is what is *next*."

"*What have you done…?*" I whisper through my fingers.

Megan crouches over the President's severed head. She tenderly runs a hand through the woman's red hair, then voices a thought. "I forgot what my hair looks like."

Winter's Doom

I'm now the one who trembles, staring down at the lifeless form of Rosella Vale, her head separated from her body, blood pouring onto the carpet like spilled wine.

I wanted this, didn't I?

Wasn't Rosella on my to-kill list?

Didn't I swear I'd kill her the next time I saw her?

Then why do I feel so terrible right now? Why do I feel like a monster? Why do I feel so sick?

"My brother can rest in his Final Peace now." Megan gives Rosella's ruby red hair one last look, then gazes up at me. There is an eerie softness in her Green Eye—which is the only eye I seem to look at now when she talks to me. "There is still … something wrong, Winter."

I flinch. "W-Wrong?"

"I know what a Warlock Stone can do. I know how to touch, manipulate, and drive the very *Anima* that enters and departs our bones—Living and Dead alike. I was once capable of so much with my Warlock Stone … which you refer to as my Green Eye. But …"

She squints with an odd and faraway expression, as if her gaze stretches deep into an ancient, unknowable past.

She shakes her head. "I feel as if my powers are not yet freed. Something holds me back. I should be able to turn all the Living of this city into Dead with just a blink of my Eye … yet it eludes me. Why is that, Winter?"

My heart is racing.

I part my lips and shut them several times.

I can't seem to settle on how to respond to her.

What do I say?

"Do you know something that could help me?" she asks me gently, like some small girl asking her mother for help in correcting a cookie recipe. "Winter … You are the only person in all the world who would know the answer. You always had the answers. I wish I …" She presses her lips together with emotion. If the Dead were capable of tears, I wonder which of her eyes would cry it: the Dead one, or the Green. "I wish I had my Winter."

"I-I'm sorry …" I finally manage to say. "I think you're capable of so much, regardless of what that Green Eye can or can't do. Look at what you've done already. I—"

"Jennifer," Grim cuts me off.

I look at him. My eyes harden.

John, perhaps suspecting something afoot, comes up to my side protectively. He still brandishes his sword, as if an enemy remains in this room, an enemy he will need to protect me from.

Grim nods expectantly at me. "Jennifer, the words—"

"Grim," I warn him bitingly.

Megan glances at each of us, confused. "The words? What words?"

Grim comes to Megan's side—a strange and unequal mirror of myself and John. "I read a poem once," he tells us. "It was in an ancient tomb about the Beautiful Dead. It spoke of many things in its timeworn pages, but there was one thing I found of great interest ... and intrigue."

"And that is?" prompts Megan.

Grim gazes upon me. *"The Green Eye opens ... when the Yellow closes. The White has arrived."*

I lose the breath from my lungs. "Grim ..." My words are choked in my fast-tightened throat. "I said ... I told you to never ..."

Megan looks at me now, searching my face for the rest of my sentences. "Winter? You knew these words?"

"I ... I heard ... I was told I—"

"You've said some of them before," Megan realizes. *"The Green Eye opens ...* I remember those words. You said them in the tomb, back at the Necropolis where we first reunited. I never knew why, or what they mean. And now I learn that there were ... *more* words ...?" She looks almost hurt. "Winter, you concealed them from me this whole time?—your friend?"

At once, I find my backbone. "They were told to me by the same man who gave us the bomb to deliver to you—the bomb we were told was a gift of blood. Those words *cannot* be trusted."

"Professor Praun didn't know it was a bomb," says Grim at once.

I stare at him, uncomprehending.

John's body turns rigid at my side, and it's he who, in a voice low with rage, says, "You knew …?"

Grim gazes at us simply. "Professor Praun exiled me with the pair of you for one single purpose. He said I was to protect Jennifer until her time came to fulfill her fate. He aimed to unite the Living and Dead through a blood pact." He spreads his hands into a shrug. "But his plan was undermined and sabotaged by the evil government, who planted a bomb in his innocent gift."

John scoffs at that. "How are we to believe a word that comes out of your mouth?"

"Because *the Green Eye opens when the Yellow closes*," answers Grim simply. *"The White has arrived.* It is time for Jennifer to embrace her destiny, and the words don't lie."

Through the glass, the fire rises, and buildings crash to the ground, and the Living scream for their lives, and students jump out of the windows, and the Dead laugh and torment them and chase them in the streets with their rusty, iron weapons and their mania.

And Grim stands there eclipsing it all with his gangly shape, a liar since the first moment I met him.

"The Green Eye opens … when the Yellow closes," recites Megan. Her strange gaze moves to the windows, then returns to me. When the weight of the words fall upon her at last, she drops her jaw with amazement. "Of course … The Yellow Eye …"

Winter's Doom

My pulse quickens. I'm anxiously palming my lump of necrocite again. "What is it, Megan? What's … What's the Yellow Eye?"

Megan studies my face for a while, as if reading the answer to my question across it.

A shadow crawls over her Green Eye like a passing storm cloud.

Suddenly, twelve Dead appear at the doorway, the clinking of their metal armor and weapons giving them away several footsteps before they appear. They enter the room, marching in unison.

"It was one of the things I envied the most," explains Megan as she starts to circle me, "when I Rose as a Dead, long, long ago. My brother and I, both. We knew of it and dreamed of it and *longed* for it …"

Three Dead grab hold of John, prying him away from me. He protests and kicks and fights against them to no avail, then drops his broadsword with a loud metal *crash* against the floor.

"JOHN!" I cry out.

"And we *missed* it," Megan goes on, "the treasure that Undeath takes from us. Even a sip of prime blood can't bring it back, not completely. And what a beautiful sight it is … something you Living take for granted every day."

Connor has similarly been apprehended, pinned to a wall by a number of Dead, where he whimpers in fear and struggles feebly against them. John has been muscled into submission and brought to his knees, where the three big Dead hold him in place.

None of the Dead come for Grim.

"What is going on??" I cry out, furious. "Megan, you called me your leader, your queen, your sister ... yet—"

"Oh, and you will be." Megan faces me. "But first ... we must close the Yellow Eye."

I back away from her as she approaches.

Then a set of Dead arms grip me from behind, a pair of Dead I can't even see.

"LET ME GO!" I shout, fighting against them, but it's no use.

John struggles and pushes against the Dead who hold him down on his knees. "Don't touch her!" he shouts at Megan. "Don't you dare touch her!"

Grim stands by Megan's side, and it's hard to tell what he feels anymore from his eyes, which have turned to stone as he watches the scene he orchestrated unfold.

Megan stops in front of me, her sword hanging loose from her hand, still stained with the President's blood. "What I'm about to do, I do with the utmost of love in my unbeating heart. You are my dearest friend, and you are the reason I am the warrior I am today. Oh, if only my brother were here to see the real you ... if only he could have had a chance to meet the *real* Winter. But ..." She sighs with deep regret. "He is no longer here, and he never will be again."

"Please, please, Megan, don't do this …"

"Winter, you don't know this now, and you won't know this for a while, but I am helping you realize who you are. We cannot own this world if the Green Eye does not open, and the Green Eye only opens when—"

"Megan … please …" Tears are falling from my eyes suddenly. I can't even pretend to be brave anymore. I'm terrified. I have never feared death more than I do in this moment. I wish I was never born. "Please … d-don't …"

"You asked me what the Yellow Eye is. Tell me, my dear Winter, what do you see outside the glass?"

I look at the window. The bright yellow beams of the sun cut abruptly through a cloud of smoke, and I squint.

And then it hits me.

It's the sun.

I turn back to Megan. "Don't do it," I plead with her, frantic. "The Living are fragile. The Living are finite. But the Dead aren't. If you kill me, if you take the sun from me, you'll end the world."

Megan observes me for one long, lingering moment. A soft smile touches her lips as she raises her sword. "My sweet friend. When you are Raised as the person you're destined to be, you'll realize the end of the world is what we should have always wanted from the start."

I suck in air to make one last plea for my life.

Megan strikes her sword into my chest instead.

"JEN!! JEN!! NO!!" John screams as he fights against the Dead holding him back. "JEN!!"

I stare at Megan, yet don't quite see her.

Everything has turned cold suddenly.

The impossibly dark shard of necrocite drops from my hand—*thud*, to the floor.

JEN!! cries a voice far, far away. *JEN!!*

Is that John calling for me?

I try to look his way, but my knees buckle, and my eyes grow too heavy to focus.

Megan's face floats in front of mine. "You brought us here. You got us this far." She smiles. "And when you return, this world will be *yours* to rule. You will see."

It doesn't even hurt. *Shouldn't it hurt …?*

The room turns onto its side. The Dead's iron-tight grip release my arms, and I fall to the floor.

My eyes flap open. The necrocite lies on the floor before my face, except I don't recognize the dark thing. I squint at it, confused the longer I stare into its depths.

It isn't dark anymore. Something's wrong.

It's glowing white.

John appears before me, perhaps having been freed from the Dead, too. "Jennifer, no, no, no … Look at me. Jennifer, say something. Oh, no … *no, no, no …*"

Winter's Doom

The tears that spill from his eyes slowly drop on my face like rain.

I try to smile, but nothing seems to happen.

"Jen, don't let go, don't, you have to fight, fight, *fight!*" John presses his warm hands to my cold, cold wound. He keeps crying. "F-Fight, damn it!"

Something in his words gives me strength.

And at once, I experience a moment where every little piece of my life clicks into place like a puzzle, and my mind becomes absolutely, pristinely, sharply clear.

It's an unexpected moment of total clarity.

My ambitions killed me. My dreaming took me too high into the sky and burnt off my wings. My hunger for knowledge grew so great, it ate the world.

I did this to myself.

The only one left to blame is me.

"J-John," I manage, despite my voice sounding wrong, throaty, and broken. "You have to tell me who I am."

He doesn't follow, his eyes searching mine.

I can see that now. *I can see everything now.*

"When I c-c-come back ... as one of ... *them* ... I won't know. Promise you'll stay by me as best as you can, John. Promise you'll tell me who I am. Until my W-W-Waking Dream, I won't know ... Tell me who I am."

"Jennifer, don't go, please, I can't ..." John's eyes burst into water as he clings to me, terrified. "Jennifer ..."

"Tell … me …"

John's face fades.

I reach out for him with hands I no longer have.

Reach out for who?

Who was I just speaking to?

What was I trying to say?

The glorious yellow sun shines fiercely through the window past a handsome man's face, tears wetting his cheeks as he cries out at me … a glorious yellow sun. It's the only thing I know. It's the only thing there. And that sun casts its beams right at me, like a friend reaching for me with bright yellow hands. The sun shines with such furious intensity, it's as if the light itself is screaming.

But it, too, fades.

I blink with eyelids I no longer have, desperate to see that brilliant sun one more time with stubborn eyes that no longer see.

What was I trying to look at?

What was I trying to say?

It isn't bright anymore, yet it isn't dark either. It's somewhere in between … like grey, but without a name. Colorlessness. Emptiness. Nothingness.

It's not light. It's not dark. It's all just …

Just …

What was I trying to say …?

Epilogue

It's the same scene that plays over and over.

The Mayor's face.

Mari's face.

A flash of light.

Nothing.

I've seen the same scene a hundred times. A thousand times. The flash of light at the end is like lightning, except I don't believe it storms here ... wherever I am. Perhaps the flashes are merely another trick of my mind.

Much like the trick that shows me *her* face, too, now and then ... interrupting the never-ending loop of Mayor, Mari, and *flash* ...

It's Jennifer's face. Her long, flowing white hair. Her smart eyes. Her strength.

Where is my green stone? How can I see her face if I don't have my green stone?

The Mayor's face.

Mari's face.

Winter's Doom

A flash of light.

Nothing.

How many more times will I see the scene? A hundred times? A thousand times? Twenty thousand? A hundred and twenty thousand?

So much time has passed. Months, maybe. Or years, quite possibly. I don't even count how many times I've seen the scene. Numbers have no context anymore.

The Mayor's face.

Mari's face.

A flash of—"I see something …"

Wait. Was that a voice?

"Oh, yes, certainly something …"

And yes, certainly a voice.

Who are you?

Oh. That question may be better asked with a mouth, which I apparently don't have.

"Try a bit harder, please. We're having trouble …"

How do I hear them at all? Do I have ears now? Is she speaking to me, or to someone else?

Who am I hearing, anyway?

Oh, perhaps I'd know if I had eyes.

"Give him eyes," she says, as if reading my mind—or wherever these thoughts exist. "No, no, not those ones. Ugh, not one those either. Appalling! I need better ones. Yes, those! A curious color. Let's try them!"

I feel something uncomfortable—a pressure. *Pop!*

Nothing.

"Nope. Let's try a different pair. Goodness, you are all so terrible at your jobs. Sorry, I'm cranky. Let's go with those other ones. No, the other-other ones."

The Mayor's face.

Mari's face.

A flash of light.

"Nope, give me another set. Maybe the pretty ones?"

The Mayor's face.

"Try those *less* pretty ones. Yes, those ones."

Mari's face.

"Pop them into place! Careful, careful …"

A flash of light …

I open my eyes.

There is a gaping sky of greyish white glory, the usual blanket of thick fog I've come to know, gone. Standing over me and eclipsing that sky are three familiar faces. Two of them, I've been watching on loop since forever ago. Mari, her round and cheery face, and in her grasp, a whole armful of eyeballs. To her right, the ever-too-tall Mayor Damnation, who stares down at me with muted pleasure, a curl of satisfaction on her lips. The third face, I don't recognize at all.

"He's awake." Mari claps her hands together. "Oh, what a relief! I thought it'd never work!"

Winter's Doom

"Make sure it's him," states the Mayor. She nudges me with the tip of her toes. It tickles. "Can you move? Do you work? Did Mari build you right?" She leans into Mari and mumbles, *"I think you did something wrong."*

I lift a hand in front of my face to observe my own fingers. I curl them into a fist, then stretch them open, in awe. I thought I'd never have a hand again. Or eyes.

Or anything.

"Looks like he works just fine," says Mari, proud of herself. "I knew it'd be worth working on him all these years. Goodness, this was fun!"

The third unrecognizable face, I only now realize, is upside-down. Is that Mayor Damnation's friend? Was her name Truce? I don't quite remember.

Why is her head attached to her neck upside-down?

"I think he's wondering why your head is attached upside-down," mutters Damn, slightly amused.

Truce—very much *not* amused—huffs with irritation. "Because apparently, when I was rebuilt, my body didn't work with my head attached *the normal* way."

"She still sounds bitter about it," mumbles Damn.

Mari giggles at that. "Oh, it isn't so bad! Your cute curly hair looks like a beard now!"

Truce shoots her a fuming look.

The Mayor bends over to bring her face and cotton-ball hair closer. "You are one *very* lucky Dead, my boy."

"And I'm one very *talented* one," Mari adds with a giggle. "He took the longest to rebuild, since he was … well, right next to the bomb. You know, I think I could build a thousand more Dead, if I like. There are so many body parts in these ruins! Countless!"

"Yes, yes," murmurs the Mayor in her dry tone, "but there is only one of *him* …" Her eyes snap to mine. "And we need you, my lovely boy, now more than ever. It just so happens that the fate of all Livingkind rests on your small, bony little shoulders. No pressure, of course."

"No pressure," Mari agrees with a nervous snicker.

"But … does he even … remember his name …?" asks the upside-down head of Truce with a touch of reluctant distaste in her sugary voice. "How do we know he has his same mind at all? He's just … *staring* at us. How do we know this whole process actually worked?"

"Erick," I state.

The three women go silent, awestruck that I spoke.

"My name …" I clear my throat of gravel, dirt, and whatever else is caught in it. "My name …" There we go. Clear as a bell. "… is Erick."

It's then that I find my legs, and with a thought, I make them bend. I press my hands to the ground, find purchase in the chalky debris and rubble in which I was for so long buried and sleeping. My body lifts in a clumsy sort of off-balanced way.

Winter's Doom

Mayor Damn, Mari, and Truce step back, eyes wide, watching.

I lift myself off the ground slowly. The world around me is a wasteland of dust, giant chunks of cement and fire-blasted stone, and Undead appendages. With my new eyes, I gaze upon my three companions, who watch with frozen faces and held breath as I stand in place, a repaired body, a reconstructed person, a perfect work of art by Mari's standards.

"So let's give him the very quick version of the story, shall we?" offers Damnation. Then she faces me. "Four years ago, your dear, loving sister led an army to the land of the Living. Jennifer, John, East, and the one named Grim went with them."

"Poor Jennifer ..." mutters Truce, then she wrinkles her nose. "I didn't trust the likes of that *Grim* one."

"Perhaps we should mention," Mari puts in, "that we receive our information from spies who report all of these activities to us via a magical device called a 'radio'. So ... the information is only *kind of* verified. Reliable hearsay, you might say. Trustworthy rumors."

Damn continues. "Your sister conquered the land of the Living and enslaved the surviving Heart Beaters. She has been amassing an empire over there for years now."

"The rest of us who *didn't* agree with her mission or her ways," adds Truce in her pleasant, playful tone, "were left stranded *here* in the Sunless Reach with the few Living who survived. We've had to ... revive ourselves."

"And by 'revive'," Mari puts in proudly, "she means that *I* had to carefully reconstruct the broken Dead from the scraps that remain. I suspect I have a knack for it!" She giggles to herself, inspiring an annoyed upside-down look from Truce. "I was likely the luckiest of all. When the bomb exploded, it sent me flying high, high, *hiiigh* in the air, and when I landed on the other end of the city where no one's lived in centuries, why ... it was almost fun! It took me only four and a half days to find my way back!"

"'*Almost fun*' she calls this," grumbles Truce, likely still bitter that Mari was unable to attach her head properly.

"What of Jennifer?" I ask.

The question causes the three women to freeze.

They exchange looks. Mari appears sad, then covers her mouth in wonder, unsure what to say. Even Truce seems to bow her head, which looks strange considering its inverted orientation.

Damnation takes a deep, unnecessary breath, then somberly answers my question: "She has been killed."

I take in the words with a cold and knowing maturity.

It was inevitable. My sister has always wanted to bring Winter back into the world to set it right again. It's what she's been waiting all of this time for.

I feared Jennifer dying was always part of her plan.

Winter's Doom

"And until she is Raised again," Damnation resumes, "the Dead will continue to greedily consume the Living world, and unless *we few of us* put a stop to it, your sister risks destroying the planet completely. We have had no leverage to turn the tide and talk sense into your sister ... without *you*."

"Without you," agrees Mari wistfully.

Truce grunts her agreement, then offers a tiny smile that looks like a tiny frown.

"And ..." Mayor Damn grimaces, then nods my way. "Your sister, as of yet, does not know you're still alive."

I'm still not, I might reply, had I more a sense of humor right now.

Except all I think of is my sister's endless hunger for blood—in more ways than one. Vengeance. Equality. Truth. Acknowledgement.

Sunlight.

And Jennifer paid the ultimate price.

Before I can voice any of my words, more people begin to gather behind the women. Other Dead who once followed my sister. Some Dead I don't know. A trio of young Living faces I remember, even after all this time— Humans who had returned with Jennifer bearing the gift that split my body into twelve hundred unsalvageable pieces: a spritely, brooding woman with choppy hair, a giant with ample brawn, and a young boy with freckles.

"Are you ready to join us, Savage Boy?" asks Damn. "Because we are quite ready to find a way across the ocean, lead our surviving few into the New World, and save this glorious planet from your dear, clueless sister."

Mari wrings her hands, causing a *click-click-click* sound. "It would be pretty awful if he said no," she mutters as an aside to Truce. "D-Do you think he'll say no?"

But I realize, with just a short look among us, that we are not enough. Even if my sister sees me, she will be too far intoxicated by the power she's amassed over the years I've been gone. She won't be moved.

Not without a very big, very scary, and very *convincing* counter to her unchecked powers.

I give them a grateful smile and a few words: "Before we go, I … suspect we may need to make a stop first."

Mari frowns. The Mayor lifts a skeptical eyebrow.

Truce grimaces and squeakily asks, "Uh … where?"

"Oh, nowhere too important." I gaze with my strange, unfamiliar eyes into the distance. "Just to see a few old friends … whom I hoped I would never see again."

With that, I start on a slow journey across the waste, which has eroded down to a desert of sorts over the years. The shuffling footsteps at my back tell me I am not alone as my companions follow me southward toward the cusp of the dead woods and beyond.

I know they are scared.

Winter's Doom

The Mayor. Mari. Truce and the Humans.

It isn't very far through the dark, thorny woods that they realize precisely where we're headed.

To the place where this all began.

To the place where this all may someday soon end.

Jennifer ... I don't know if you can hear me.

I don't know if you can see me through some veil of Undeath, in the void that exists between being Alive and being Undead. Maybe you're already finding your way to your body once again to at last reclaim your rightful name as Winter, the queen of the Dead.

I cannot promise that my reckless plan will work in saving you and your world from the hungry, vengeance-seeking clutches of my dear, loving sister.

But of one thing I can certainly promise you: *I will see you again.*

To Be Continued ...

Daryl Banner

Did you enjoy *Winter's Doom?*

Turn the page to read the COMPLETE FIRST CHAPTER

of the final book in the Beautiful Dead saga: *Deathless*.

Chapter One
Queen Winter

I come into this world like everyone does:

Crying, apparently.

"Oh, she's awake! She's awake! And she's ... oh, dear. She's crying. Oh, Dead Heavens and Hells, what do I do?"

The words come from a woman nearby whom I can't yet see. I'm currently squinting against something bright and horrible. Is someone flashing a light in my face? What is that terrible, awful light?

"Come, come! The day's here at last! Dead Heavens, it's here at last! And bring tissues! She'll burn her face off if she keeps up with these tears!"

Are my eyes even open?

I don't know, but they sure do burn.

One woman's voice is traded for another's: a softer voice, a kinder, sweeter voice. "Oh, my. It's true," she says through the angry haze behind which I'm apparently trapped. "Can you hear me, sweetheart? Can you see me? Follow my voice. Look for me."

"I … I can't," I cry out, confused—and I'm startled at once by the sound of my own voice. *Was that my voice??*

A soft tissue touches my cheek suddenly.

I swat at it, annoyed.

"There, there …" she speaks again, even softer. "No more tears. None are needed. Today is a day of *celebration*, my dear friend. Today is *your* day!"

I'm desperately reaching for something, yet I don't know what it is. A name? A face? An answer to something important?

Name … What's my name? Shouldn't I know?

"Your name is Winter," she answers, as if she held the answer over my head and was merely waiting for me to think the question. "You're Undying, my sweet, beautiful friend, and it will all be finished soon."

Dying? Did she just say I'm dying?

Why do I feel like I just woke from a nap, yet can't for the life of me remember what the hell I was doing before I laid myself down? It's like waking suddenly from a lovely dream, yet not being able to remember falling asleep to dream in the first place—nor what I dreamed at all.

"Take my hand. Squeeze it firmly. You'll know you exist when you feel the touch of my—"

At once, soft skin settles upon my smooth, sensitive, dry-as-sand palm.

It feels … pleasant. *I think.*

Deathless

"Good, good. Some of us call that our First Hand. It's a term I'm trying to bring back," she adds cutely to her friend, who titters, as if at some private joke I don't get. "Ah, I've been a Crypter for so long, I forget where even half the words come from. How is my hand? Is it soft?"

I don't move, nor do I answer the woman.

I just lie there in eerie, floating nothingness, with the gentle touch of her skin on my palm.

"You're doing lovely, by the way. Now squeeze."

I sit up instead.

"Wait, slow, slow, not too fast, Winter. You must take your time. This is all going to be very new to you."

"I'm ..." My own voice stuns me again, like a loud bell made of diamond ringing in my ears. "I-I'm ... Winter ...? Why am I blind? I can't see—"

"Give it time. Your eyes are adjusting, and soon ..."

She doesn't finish the words before at once, the whole world comes into focus before me.

A young woman, bald, one dark eye, one green eye that glows, her eyes different sizes, a tiny nose, a sweet lopsided smile, her body cloaked in a long green gown.

I blink at her. What a peculiarly strange set of eyes.

"My name is Megan," she introduces herself. "And your name is Winter. I am here to help you through this."

The lady next to her is another sweet-faced, gentle-looking thing with black hair cropped strictly at her chin, and a pointy nose. She has a stiff smile painted over her angular face, and she seems incapable of blinking. "H-Hi," she greets me quietly, then offers nothing else.

I peer around me. I'm in a small, fancy bed chamber of sorts. I've sat up from a mattress with black, silken sheets poured over it like thick smoke. Before me stands a great window that overlooks a vast, sprawling city, which glows molten red, as if the whole of it is set afire.

"Is this Hell?" I ask politely.

Megan lets out a musical laugh. "This is your home. It's called New Necropolis." She squeezes my hand, then brings her face close to mine. "And you are its queen."

I blink.

Wait. What?

"Queen Winter," says the other lady, her voice nearly bubbling with mirth. "We've been waiting for you for so, so long."

"How long?" I ask, looking at each of them with big, troubled eyes. "I've been asleep? Why can't I remember anything? Do I have ..." I gasp. *Do I have amnesia?*

The women look at each other. "I ... don't know what that is," admits Megan, then smiles apologetically at me. "But I think all your questions will be answered soon. You must have patience."

"I'm a queen?"

"Yes. Queen of New Necropolis. Well, soon."

Deathless

Queen …

Shouldn't I know if I'm a queen?

"Come." Megan rises off the bed and tugs upon my hand, which she still firmly grasps.

I rise from the bed, too, then cross the room toward the window with her. Through its glass, I peer out at the vast city below. The buildings, in fact, are not on fire; they stand tall and proud, and they appear to be made of glass and metal. It is the flames of torches and braziers lining the streets that shine their shimmery red and orange hues upon the buildings, making them look afire.

Oh, there's a multitude of greens in the flames, too.

And five tones of violet.

And ten separate hues of orange.

And twelve hundred shades of sapphire.

Goodness gracious. "I … I never knew fire to be so … so *colorful*," I catch myself saying, shocked.

"She's handling this quite well," observes the other lady to Megan.

"Yes," Megan agrees happily. "She is."

I gaze down below and find people walking the streets of the city. That's when I notice that some of them are dressed in very little clothing and thick iron collars around their necks. Chain leashes are attached to them, and they are being tugged along by other people like pet dogs.

"Who—Who are they?" I ask, concerned.

Megan comes to my side, then nods with somber understanding. "Servants of the Dead."

"D-Dead ...?"

"I only just told you, remember?" Megan turns me away from the window. "You are Undead now. Queen of the Undead. Of New Necropolis. The Unliving Queen."

"And ..." I glance back at the window. "The ones who wear the chains ... they are our servants?"

Megan chuckles at my piecing together of thoughts. "You've got it. Servants of the Dead, yep."

"Oh." I feel sad for them suddenly. I bring a hand instinctively to my chest, as if wondering if my heart might slow with sadness for them—until I realize there's nothing beating in my chest at all.

Then a question occurs to me. "So *they* aren't Dead?"

"Them? The servants?" Megan titters, finding that amusing somehow. "No. That's why they serve us."

I stare out the window, observing a young, nearly-naked man in chains being tugged unkindly along by a larger, clothed man, who looks too impatient for his own good. "Well, I sure hope they're being paid a ... a decent living wage," I note, "because otherwise, that's cruelty, and someone ought to do something about that."

The women share another look. Then Megan gives my back a gentle pat and says, "In time, you will see."

"I will see what?"

Deathless

"That they are where they are for a reason, and they deserve their fate." Megan shakes her head with pity at the glass. "It wasn't too long ago that us *Dead* were the ones who were treated cruelly ... like vermin, like trash, cast away to the other side of the world. Both the Undead *and* our Living sympathizers were treated terribly."

I gaze out the window, uncertain.

Megan lifts her mismatched eyes up to meet mine, and a look of peaceful resolve makes them sparkle. "My sweet Winter. Today is a very special day, didn't I tell you? And it will answer your ultimate question directly: *Who are you?*" She smiles warmly. "Oh, but when you find out ... I can't wait!" She giggles like a giddy little girl, which inspires a giggle of delight from her pointy-nosed friend. "Come, my queen. I'll show you around the city. Everyone has been *dying* to meet you." Megan nudges me. "Get it? *Dying?* Oh, we're going to have *so much fun*, Winter! It'll be just like old times!"

Suddenly, the other one offers a polite objection. "Do you think we're ... going too fast for her?" She wrings her hands uncertainly and winces apologetically at Megan. "I mean, I've waited a long, *long* time for this day to come, just like you, but maybe we're—"

"No." Megan takes me by the hand. "We're not going too fast. Winter here can keep up." She turns her odd eyes to me. "Can't you, Winter?"

I'm not certain about anything. I don't know what's going on. Shouldn't I know simple things? Like where I came from? Or how I can possibly walk around while not having air in my lungs or blood in my heart? Shouldn't I know my own name without someone telling me it?

Instead of any of that, I just answer: "Yes."

"Good," chirps Megan, then leads me out of the room.

I feel like I'm walking ten steps behind myself as she takes me through a twisting web of hallways, then down a long flight of stairs. The building is a palace of some kind with dark, ornate walls, decorative fixtures, strong iron stairs and banisters, elaborate lanterns every step of the way, and many, many tall stained-glass windows.

Is this my palace?

Is this where I live …?

Megan shows me what she calls "the library wing", which is an enormous circular, wooden room with walls full of books. She boasts of how many tens of trillions of words must fill this great library. "All of it, yours," she sings cheerily as she shows me around.

I smile mutedly and drink in the view.

That's a lot of Sunday morning books to read.

Megan shows me a sprawling auditorium where we entertain each other with rehearsed performances in my honor. "My honor …?" I ask her, but she only quiets me and urges me to pay attention as she continues the tour.

Deathless

I'm shown our treasure stores—a long and narrow stone chamber made of bluish-grey brick where a heap of gold and shimmery things, oddities, relics, and other worthy keepsakes are held. I'm also shown a ball room where lavish dances and parties are hosted. I'm shown a weapons room, an armory, a utility and inventions and advancements room, a playroom for the young ones, a museum, a gymnasium, an afternoon sitting room, a midnight sitting room, a dining hall fit for a hundred guests, a second gymnasium, more weapons rooms, another armory, a hall of bedrooms, a powder parlor …

All of this fits in my palace.

I have to catch my breath—only to be reminded anew that I have none.

"No Undead have been born since you left," Megan tells me as she takes me into the streets at last, the view of the enormous five-story palace falling at my back. "We have had many debates about it, but I believe you are the reason the Dead Rise. See, my Green Eye has shown me many powers over the years, and I've been able to, with a great effort, Raise the Living into Dead—or at least those whom we deem worthy," she adds quickly.

A couple of Dead pass us by, their chained servant—a mud-spackled young woman with almondy skin and sad eyes wearing nothing but a black bra and skirt—trailing behind them, struggling to keep up.

The sight pains me. "You said 'we' have had debates about it …? Who is 'we'?"

Megan nods. "Of course, I hadn't told you yet. Your Council. It is made up of some very trusted advisors who will help you in ruling New Necropolis. Today is a special day, I told you."

"Yes, yes," I agree with muted annoyance as we pass yet another pair of a righteous, proudly clothed Dead and his scraps-for-clothing servant: a handsome man with dirt caking his feet, huffing and puffing as he follows along.

"So I hope, with your return, that more Dead will Rise from the ground as they once did in your presence."

"I … used to Raise the Dead?" I ask, astonished.

Megan only laughs, rubs my back, and continues guiding me along.

The streets are far more populated than the big five-story mansion I've been sleeping in all this time. Nearly each person who passes by seems to recognize me. Some stop in their tracks, as if shocked by my presence. Others immediately bow or kneel before me with: "My queen!" Others stare at me in drooling disbelief, their servants forced to stop and watch me too.

We arrive at a large parlor, where two powdery-faced women with giant eyes greet me. "I will leave you here for now," Megan tells me. "These lovely ladies will be freshening you up for your coronation."

Deathless

I stare at Megan. "C-Coronation?"

"Yes, of course. That's why today is a big day!" She gently takes me by the shoulders, then leans in. "Today, you are being formally crowned before all the citizens of New Necropolis as their Queen Winter."

Too stunned to speak, I simply stare at her as if she didn't say anything at all.

Megan gives me a light nudge toward the door. "Go on, then, Winter. This was always your favorite part." She steps aside with her pointy-nosed friend, and it's now the two powdery-faced women who guide me into the building. My eyes linger on Megan's. "I'll see you soon!" she promises me cheerily.

Then quite suddenly, I'm sat before a mirror, except my chair is forced to face away from it while the ladies start fussing over me, asking about choices in the color of my queenly gown, while the other combs my long white hair into submission.

"Don't worry," murmurs one of the ladies in a lofty, melodic tone. "The years of deathly slumber have ... well, they've made a tangle or two. Would you like an up-do, or a down-do, or a whole new style entirely?"

"I suggest the crimson one," the other lady says to me, presenting a dress, "but of course we also have azure ..."

"Perhaps a decorative ornament set about your hair, like a landmark among a snowdrift?" comes the other.

"I could fetch you dresses in hues of emerald, if you so desire instead," comes the other.

"Maybe pearls set right here in your hair? Or here? Or over here? Or nowhere at all, of course, whichever."

"A pearl dress, perhaps? Or is that too much white?"

Their questions come like gunfire.

Gunfire.

I flinch from the word, terrified by it somehow.

"Oh ... D-Did I say something wrong?" asks the lady with the dresses, worried.

"It was me," decides the other lady, fretting. "I pushed you too much about your hair. Don't worry. You'll look amazing no matter what you choose, of course."

"I ..." It's the first word I've uttered since I stepped foot into this place. "I ... don't mind. You both can ... can choose whatever. I don't mind any of it at all."

My words are flat and unconvincing.

Perhaps Megan's mousy friend was right.

Perhaps this all too much, too quickly.

The ladies, clearly oblivious to my inner plight, set to doing my hair and dressing my body. Despite all of the fuss they made in choosing all the right options, the ordeal of fixing me up seems to take all of two minutes.

Then I'm spun about, and at once I face a woman.

I think the woman is supposed to be me.

But I don't know her.

Deathless

"Do you like it?" asks the hair lady, cooing. "Oh, tell me you adore it, please!" begs the dress lady.

I stare at my reflection, paralyzed.

Is that what I look like?

I'm lost in the strange, slender shape of my deathly pale face, the narrow bridge of my small nose, my sunken cheeks, my colorless lips, my shadowy blue eyes that look more like crystalline decorations than they do actual eyes, like a doll's, fit for a display shelf. My shaped, pencil-thin eyebrows arch to express my bewilderment—and it's so strange an experience, to watch a woman's eyebrows go up at just the same moment you lift your own, and not recognizing that the woman is you in the mirror.

Is this anything like how I looked ... before?

Or is this a completely new person?

"W-Winter?" The powder ladies are getting worried. "Is everything alright? Should we call Megan back ...? *I think we broke her,*" she whispers to her partner suddenly. "*Yes, maybe,*" her partner agrees anxiously. "*We shouldn't have shown her the mirror so soon. Rookie mistake.*"

"I'm fine," I announce suddenly, coming to. I feel like I'm out of breath, like a panic attack is coming on. Is that possible if you don't even breathe? "I ... I think I ..."

I spot a small door in the corner. That must be the restroom, certainly.

"I need a bathroom break, if you ladies don't mind."

As if I just spoke some accursed, banished word, the two ladies look at one another, wide-eyed, then back at me, frozen in place.

I offer them a smile of apology. "Sorry. Nature calls."

"She's acting like a Trentonite," mumbles the dress lady to the other. *"Do we play along ... or ...?"*

"Of course," says the hair lady to me, a broad smile spreading her powdery face apart. She gestures at the door. "A moment's privacy, you are afforded whenever you so wish. Take your time. We'll be waiting here when you're ready to be escorted back to the palace, of course."

I give them both as polite a smile as I can manage, then make my way for the small door. I open it, slip inside the bathroom, then shut it with an unnecessary sigh.

It's a bathroom, though it doesn't appear to be used as one; the toilet is empty of water and filled instead with a lot of tiny canisters of colors, and the sink has small boxes stacked upon it filled with tiny hair ornaments, bows, and plastic clips of every color.

Across from the door is a window.

I bite my lip, staring at that window long and hard.

"Winter ...?" comes the voice of the hair lady from the other side of the door. "Are you alright, my dear?"

The longer I stare at that window, the less alright I feel. The more quickly I'm ushered from one task to the next, the less alright I feel.

Deathless

Quite suddenly, I'm not alright at all.

"W-Winter ...?" she calls again.

At once, I charge toward the window and thrust it open with ease. I lift the skirt of my red dress, throw a leg over the sill of the window, and awkwardly shove my way out of it.

On the streets now, I hurry away in the first direction that captures my interest. To the right, I go. I pass many faces who seem surprised at my appearance. I don't look at any of them, too spooked for manners and politeness. I hurry past an orchard that's fenced in by iron posts and wire, within which several near-naked servants labor.

High above me, eclipsed only by the tallest of nearby buildings, I see a wash of grey for a sky, no sun to be found at all—just grey, grey, grey.

What time is it? Why does peering into the sky tell me nothing, except for perhaps a forecast of possible rain?

I pass a spread of storefronts and unnamed buildings and countless more shocked faces. "Winter?" comes one of them. "Is that ... the queen?" asks another, astonished. "Winter! It's Winter! Winter has awakened!" "Wiiinter!"

Wiiinter ... Wiiinter ...

I realize I have to get off the streets.

As if answering my prayers, I spot a dark alley set between a blacksmith's shop and a bakery, and in that alleyway, a pair of cellar doors.

I pry them open and, unseen, plunge down the dark flight of stairs, letting the doors slam shut above me.

My eyes adjust immediately somehow, and even in the perfect dark, I see the wooden edge of every step as I descend into the basement of … wherever this is.

At the foot of the stairs, I stop, and gaze out before me at the dark, curious room.

There are tall shelving units all over, filled with bottles of oddly-colored liquids, powders, and chunks of stone. I find a stack of broken weapon parts—handles to axes, hilts of swords, shattered blades, long metal rods.

For all my boasting a second ago about how lovely my eyesight is down here, it's a wonder my foot doesn't see the metal chalice on the ground—which it promptly kicks on accident, sending the thing careening deeper into the basement.

The clatter of its echoes fill the room, then die as it settles somewhere unseen.

Then I hear movement.

I stop. The movement stops, too.

It comes from around the corner of the wall. Slowly, I approach. My stupid crimson gown makes stealth nearly impossible, for all the annoying *crunching* and *swishing* of fabric this gown causes as I move along.

When I come around the corner, the tip of a blade appears at my face.

Deathless

I lift my hands at once, alarmed.

The tip of the blade is all I see, hovering before me.

"Sorry," I say to the blade. "I … I got lost. I didn't … I didn't mean to invade your private space. I'm sorry. I—"

The blade slowly lowers.

In its place, I now see the handsome face of a man. He has warm brown eyes that sparkle somehow, even in the darkness. He has a head of short-cropped messy brown hair and a dark trimmed beard that compliments his thick blunt eyebrows, which now lift in surprise. He wears a fitted pair of brown pants that disappear into a set of thick boots, with nothing but a vest hung loosely over his bare, muscled chest. His arms reveal the strength of his body, the musculature apparent at first sight.

The tip of his blade touches the ground. His eyes don't leave my face as he stares at me in disbelief, his full, plush lips parted.

I'm taken at once by his handsomeness. I mean, if we're being honest here, the brawny man standing before me is stunning by all definitions of the word. I'd even say he's beautiful in his own way.

That's when I notice the metal collar around his neck.

Servant. He is someone's servant.

"Sorry," I say once more. "I got lost, like I said. I'll … I'll find my way out. Carry on with what you're doing. I'll just—" My eyes drop down to his muscled chest. I flinch and pull my gaze away. *Goodness, can I contain myself for a moment?* "Sorry. Good day. Or whatever it is. I can't tell. The sky is just grey. Goodbye." I turn to leave, hurrying along toward the stairs.

Then, over my head, a light appears, filling the room.

I stop in surprise, then turn back around.

The man stands by a light switch on the wall, which he just flicked on. His stunned stare is upon me all over again, except now, his breathing has changed.

A single tear escapes from his eye. It draws a long path down his cheek and disappears into his beard.

I stare at him, taken once more by his presence.

Then he says: "Is … Is that really you …?"

I try to remember myself and give him a polite smile. "Yes. It's me. Apparently everyone knows me."

A flicker of doubt passes over his face. "Everyone …?"

I shrug. "I've been bowed at, kneeled at, and greeted by nearly every person I passed on the street. So, yes. I'm the queen … or whatever. I just …" I glance behind me at the stairs that lead up to the cellar doors. "I just needed to get away from it for a moment, I guess."

When I return my gaze to him, I find the man three steps closer, his eyes wide and drinking me in.

Then he says: "Jennifer."

I frown, confused. "Who?"

"Jennifer. That's your name. Y-You're Jennifer … Jen."

Deathless

I stare at him in bewilderment. "My name is Winter," I respond—using a piece of knowledge I only minutes ago learned as if it's absolute fact.

"No, you're not," he insists. "You're Jennifer Steel. You and I ..." He appears pained for a moment, as if the words he says wound him somehow. "You made me swear to stay by your side. I tried, Jen. I tried as ... as best as I could after they killed you, but—"

I gape at him. "Killed me?"

"Yes. Megan. Grim. The Dead. They killed you. They ended your Life and gave you *this* one."

My eyes are cast to the floor in shock.

Megan? Who's Grim? *This can't be true.*

"They pulled us apart after you died," he goes on to tell me, his voice tense with emotion. "They took me far away from you and did with me what they did with all the other survivors. Made us into slaves. Well ..." He gives a gesture at himself. "Some of us were treated better than others. Maybe because Megan knew my connection to you, or ... I don't know."

"Connection?"

He takes another step toward me. "We were students here, you and I. It was so long ago, Jennifer ... the war, the great war between the Living and the Dead. We lost. The Living, I mean. You and I helped the Dead invade this land on a hovercraft. This city that you call New

Necropolis … it used to be Skymark University. And you and I … We … We were …" He grits his teeth as his eyes shimmer with emotion. "W-We were in love, Jen."

I take a step back from him.

"No, don't be scared, please, don't run away. You told me to stay by your side. Right before you died, you told me to stay by your side and remind you who you were— to tell you everything. Here I am, at last, at *long* last fulfilling that promise. It's been five long years since that day. You are Jennifer Steel. You have a mother in the countryside who—I pray every day—is still alive and well and *free* from the Dead's reach of power, which grows farther and stronger every passing day. The government is collapsed. The Living have lost control of this land. The Dead rule the world now. Jennifer …"

"Please stop calling me that," I ask him curtly, taking another step backward.

My heel kicks into the foot of the wooden stairs.

"Okay." He takes a jagged breath. "O-Okay."

"My name is Winter," I state again. "I told you that."

"Yes, right." He huffs with frustration, takes another breath, then gazes up at me. "W … Winter. I know things are very confusing. You were told one thing, now I'm telling you another. You warned me this would happen. Until you have your Waking Dream, your memory won't come back on its own."

Deathless

"Waking Dream …?"

"Yes. All the Undead have them. Your whole previous life will come back to you in one sudden instant. You told me all about them." A lightness returns to his face. "You taught me nearly everything I know about the Dead. You studied them here at Skymark, in fact."

Quite suddenly, I sit down on the step behind me, though I can't be sure whether I meant to sit down, or merely collapsed with grace.

My head spins.

Who do I trust …?

"I know, I'm going too fast. I'm sorry." He sighs as he crouches right there on the floor, wringing his hands. "I shouldn't … I shouldn't push you to remember. There is no sense in that. Your Waking Dream will come when it's time for it to come, but …" His pretty brown eyes, still wet with tears of astonishment, soften as they meet mine. "Just know, if you're ever lost, you have a friend here. A real, honest friend … possibly your last true one left."

I stare at the floor, his words sinking in.

What reason would some random servant have to lie to me like this? His words are too personal to be made up. His urgency, his reaction, his emotion … too intense.

Too intense to not be real.

Is my name really Jennifer Steel? Was I really killed? By Megan? And someone called Grim …?

"How do I …" I decide to put him on the spot. Why not? I'm to be the queen soon, aren't I? "How do I know you're telling the truth?"

He gives it a second's thought. Then, with a lift of his eyebrows, he gives me an answer. "Birthmark. At the base of your back, left side. A birthmark the shape of a sword that's missing half its handle."

The cellar doors open at once, and a large man's voice booms down the stairs. "John, your assistance is needed with fifteen orders for blades! The Royal Army requires that we—" He notices me with a start. "Oh. M-My queen. Is that you? Is that—?"

"Yes," I decide, rising from the step and turning to face him. "It is I, Queen Winter of New Neanderthal."

The man's face wrinkles up. "New … what?"

Oh, did I get the name wrong? "New N-Necropolis, like I said," I amend with faux annoyance.

The man nods apologetically. "Of course, my queen. I clearly misheard. I'm … I'm sorry to have, ah, yelled so brazenly in your, ah, ah, in your presence." He clears his throat. Then, in a far more dignified tone, he says, "John. Please come to perform your assigned duties."

The handsome man with which I've been speaking— John by name, apparently—walks past me. His eyes linger on my face, soft and brown and watery with feeling, as he passes by. I keep my gaze on his, my heart melting within as he ascends the stairs, and too soon, they are gone, and I'm left staring up at the opened cellar doors, alone.

What a strange first day as a Dead this has been.

A mere five minutes later, to my surprise, I find my way back to the palace, where a very high-strung Megan awaits me. "Goodness, I thought something terrible had happened to you!" she exclaims upon my arrival, swiftly ushering me back into the palace. "The ladies at the salon swore you were just taking a small bathroom break, then find you've escaped through the window! Where did you go, my queen? Why did you run away?"

"I just ... needed some air," I answer lamely.

Megan exercises a very visible moment of calming herself down. "Well, I ... suppose that's understandable," she decides.

"It is," I agree as we ascend a winding staircase.

"Yes, good. How about we prepare for your big day? The members of your esteemed Council will meet with you soon—once you're officially crowned and *ready*, of course—and we will quickly decide on—"

"I need a moment," I announce, stopping in front of the doors to the library.

Megan eyes the doors with suspicion. "Is this another attempt to run away? Really, Winter, at this rate, we'll *never* get that crown on your head, and we only have—"

"Just one moment. I won't run."

"Winter ..."

I thrust myself through the doors and shut them at my back. My eyes scan the round, wooden library for a thing I noticed before.

A tall, narrow mirror, fixed between two bookshelves.

I rush up to that mirror, for a moment feeling as if some strange woman is rushing toward it from the other side, not recognizing myself. I stand before it in my deep crimson gown and perfectly-placed white hair.

Well, there's no easy way to do this, really.

I attempt to shrug off my dress, then find my intended maneuver impossible to complete. With a huff, I start to hike the whole crimson gown upward, thinking I'd slip it off over my head, only to find myself tangled in its silky red fabrics, grunting as I struggle to free myself from it. I make many unflattering sounds and contort myself in all possible directions before, at last, the dress slips off of my body and pours onto the floor in a pile of reddish silk.

Now in just my underwear, I slowly turn my back toward the mirror while peering over my shoulder.

Right there, at the small of my back, left side, is a tiny birthmark.

The shape of a sword.

Missing half its handle.

I gasp.

The next moment, Megan enters the room. "Winter!"

Deathless

I turn to her. "Um ..."

Megan sighs, slaps a hand to her forehead ... and then finds herself laughing. "Oh, really, though. It's been so long since we've been together and ..." She laughs again, despite herself. "This really *is* very Winter-like behavior."

I blink. "It is?"

"No worries. I'll fix you right back up myself. Just a bit of an adjustment to your hair, and helping you get your dress on, and ... Well, let's just get to it." Megan comes right up to me, then slowly starts to help me back into my dress and fix my hair back up.

And all the while, I keep catching my blank eyes in the mirror, and John's words circle my mind, over and over.

Then, quite suddenly, and without my full permission, the question bursts out of me: "Who is John?"

All of Megan's tugging on my dress stops.

Her whole face stops, in fact.

I wonder if the entire planet stopped spinning at my uttering of that one seemingly simple question.

"H-How did you ..." Megan's voice is nearly a hiss. "How did you hear his name ...?"

I turn to face her, alarmed by the abrupt reaction. "So you know him?"

Megan's lips slowly close. Then her eyes narrow with suspicion. Then, after ten more emotions seem to have their way with her face, she at last says, "I was ... hoping to be able to tell you such things at the right time. Not on this day. Not … so soon."

"He's a Living, isn't he?" I ask, pushing her to tell me more. "That would mean that he's a servant?"

"Yes," answers Megan plainly.

I study her face a moment longer. "And do you like him?"

It's now that a different variety of emotion falls on Megan's face. She doesn't look uncomfortable. Or angry. Or defensive. In fact, it's a wistful look of affection that now softens her eyes.

She smiles, then finally gives me a confirming nod.

I lift an eyebrow. "Do … I like him?"

Megan lets out one soft chuckle, then smirks.

Her reaction isn't quite an answer. "So … is that a yes? A maybe? A definitely not?"

After a moment's pause, she reaches out and takes my hand. "It's too complicated an answer to give right now. Whatever you were told of him, I assure you, there are several sides to the story, and in time, you will know each and every one of them. You'll know about the war. You'll know about who you were … and John. You will know about what it cost us all to get here."

I wonder if one of those costs was my life.

I wonder if she'll tell me someday how she killed me.

Perhaps that'll be a chat we have over cups of tea.

Deathless

"But now isn't the time, my friend." She offers me a smile. "The city awaits. Are you ready to be crowned in front of the world, the Queen of New Necropolis, Queen of the Undead, the Unliving Queen, Queen Winter?"

To all those titles, to all the pomp, to the grand spread of her hands and to all the glamor in her words, I merely shrug. "Sure."

Megan's face falters.

I guess a little more enthusiasm couldn't hurt.

In a matter of hours, I'm standing before a great red curtain that separates me from a balcony on the top floor of my palace. Beyond that balcony, a vast courtyard is filled with every citizen and servant—Living *and* Dead— who reside in our great city.

I stare at the back of the curtain and listen to the murmurs of the crowd. Unlike before, I feel a prickling sense of impending … something. I'm not sure what it is I'm about to face, but I'm excited for it to come.

Really, who can say they wake up with no recollection of who they are, only to find that they're to be crowned Queen of the Dead?

"Do you have a servant of your own?" I ask Megan as she troubles over my gown, ensuring each and every fold looks lovely and pristine.

Megan smiles. "I do, but Grim is a *special* servant."

Grim.

That's the name of the other one who killed me, according to John.

"He deserves the dignity of clothes," Megan goes on, "and his own bed chambers here in the palace, regular *Human* meals … and my undying respect, of course. It was thanks to him—*and you*—that the Dead were able to conquer this land, which is rightfully ours."

"I think I'd like to have a servant, too," I tell her.

"Oh, Winter." She finds that hilarious. "The whole *world* is your servant. *I'm* your servant. You're the queen."

"But I want a *special* servant. Like yours." I face her. "A servant who has their own bed chambers here in my palace, too. Someone …"

Someone I can trust.

I don't finish that sentence.

Instead, I say: "Someone … like John."

There is a long spell of silence after my words. Megan hosts a war across her face as she struggles for a response. Then, at long last, she merely gives in with a, "That can be arranged, I do think."

"Good." I smile with relief, then face the curtain.

Gently, Megan smooths out the front of my gown, touches something in my hair, then meets my eyes. "Are you ready to take on the world now, my Winter?"

I wonder if I have ever been more *not* ready for something as I am now.

Deathless

"You bet I am," I answer anyway.

Toward the curtains I'm ceremoniously brought, and when they are pulled aside by a pair of armored guards, a chorus of cheering and shouting flood my ears like the crashing of great ocean waves. I stand at the edge of the balcony, facing the thousands upon thousands of people I now rule.

Upon a velvety pillow, crimson as blood, a crown is brought to me. It is a delicate tiara set with tiny green and yellow gems. At its front, a great white stone is fixed, and the stone glows and surges with energy.

It's as if the thing has a pulse of its own.

The crown is placed on my head, and before me, yet another wave of merry screams and cheers crash through the crowds.

Quite suddenly, I wonder if I *am* ready for this.

Should I request another day?

Ask politely for a postponement?

Thank the crowd for coming, but asking them to please return tomorrow when I'm feeling slightly less freaked out?

"Meet your Queen!" cries Megan through a system, which amplifies her voice tenfold, throwing it out to the people and shaking the buildings around us. "Queen of New Necropolis, Queen of the Dead, the Unliving Queen, Queen of the world … Your Queen Winter!"

But now, I find it's far too late to stop the process. It is already here, spread before me in a crowd of countless cheering faces who stand far, far below me.

Maybe it doesn't matter at all, whatever worries lie unresolved in my chest. Maybe I can feel taller than the world for a while … if I like. I can be immortal. I can be all-powerful.

In fact, I feel strangely capable of anything now.

They cheer my name. They revere me.

They worship me, Queen of the Dead, ruler of the world, Queen Winter …

Whoever she is.

Join "Daryl's Doorway" on Facebook
and be the very first to hear news about the final book in
the Beautiful Dead saga: *Deathless*.
www.facebook.com/groups/DarylsDoorway
